STRAIGHT TO The POINT BOOKS
P R E S E N T S

Women Are Dogs Too...

Like Daughter,
Nothing Like Mother...

a novel

By

Antoinette Smith

STTP Books
Riverdale, GA

Published in the U.S.A. by
Straight to the Point Books
Riverdale, Georgia

Copyright © 2015 by Antoinette Smith

ISBN: 1-930231-56-3 / 978-1-930231-56-6

Editor: Windy Goodloe
Cover Design: Marion Designs
Interior Book Layout: The Rod Hollimon Company

Printed in the United States of America

Acknowledgements

I would like to, first and foremost, thank God for giving me the ability to write. Not only did He give me a gift and a talent, He also gave me the strength to speak up about my past and help others in pain as well. I strongly believe that God has a purpose for everyone's life.

I have to thank my Dream Team— Mr. Rod Hollimon, my publisher/friend; Ms. Windy Goodloe, my excellent editor/friend; and Mr. Keith Saunders, book cover designer.

I have to give thanks to my God-Mommy (Myola Smith) and my God-Daddy (Mr. Dennis Pete). I want to thank you two for the never-ending motivation that you give me and the unconditional love that I feel from you guys.

I would like to thank my fans for believing in me. I would like to also thank my fans for keeping me lifted, by letting me know that they are indeed looking forward to my next book.

I would like to give a special thanks to Ocean's 66 in College Park, Big Daddy's Catering, Wheels and Tires by Johnnie Bailey.

I would also like to give a special thanks to my Mexican family at El Ranchero Mexican restaurant in College Park. I will list all of their names because they are all very special to me, so here goes... George, Robert, Nacho, Penguin, Cheo, Alicia, Luis, Juan Luis, Crilin, Chava, Elias a.k.a Fred Flintstone, Sulvador, Memo, Joaquin, Cesar, Gus, Paco, El Jaliskillo, Antonio a.k.a Harry Potter, Jackie Chan, Nasa, That Red Bitch, Tifany, a.k.a Girl Power, Daniel, Christian, Danielle & Maria (we miss you),Beto, Chunga, Negro, Miguel, Chuto, Wicho, Hugo, Tito, Zorro, Gilles Saint-Germain, and Cacheton.

I would also like to thank Blue and his Dark Blue Security Team— Rico_Strong, Tee, Cedric Williams, and Tawan.

I would also like to thank the College Park Police Department.

I can't forget to give a special thanks to my baby Dee!!"

I have to say…if it wasn't for pain, I wouldn't be who I am today. Sometimes pain is good, so don't look at it as a bad thing.

To my kids, who are known as my 5 Lights, I write for you, for us— Pinky! Driah! Clyde! Chicken! Fat Boy!

I meant it when I said that I would write us out of the hood… I love you all so much!

I would like to also thank Lupe and his crew at El Nopal Mexican Restaurant

You Only Need One Person to Believe in You and That's You!

Antoinette Smith

A Special Dedication

To My Loved Ones and Friends Who are Gone Too Soon and Most Definitely Never Forgotten…

Hattie Lee Reid Pearson

Oscar Pearson

Vurilyn Toon

Harry Pearson

Willie Pearson

Lucile Brown

Arthur Brown

Nelson "Hump" Redmon

Tremeesa "Rat" West

Yvonne "Sister" Walker

Claudette McGhee

Willie McGhee

Patricia Ann Walker

Sabrina "Shawn" Murphy

Carrie Mae Wilson

Kathy "Kitty Kat" Carter

Daryl Carter

Acie "Hubbard" Wilson

Pearline Strowder

Catherine "Dot Dee" Simpson

Robin Lynn Jones

Devorris "DMoss" Moss

Beth Nicole "Candygurl" Dodson

Omar "O" Jerrod Brown

Ronald Jerome Holston

Michael Jackson

Whitney Elizabeth "Nippy" Houston

Trayvon Martin

Ms. Jeanette Wright

Annette Jones

Willie Frank Webb, Jr

Trevion Davis

Mr. Kwik

God picks special flowers,
and these are a few that He added to His Heavenly Garden.

From the Twisted Mind of a Gemini

Please don't judge me, love me.
And don't feel sorry for me, pay me.
All you want is the honey,
And all i want is the money.
Some people love me, and some people hate me,
But, in the end, i can only be me.
I love doing whatever i want when i want,
And let's face it, i get whatever i want.
This is my life and one hell of a story,
And no one can fit my shoes, so don't worry.
I love this perfect life that i live,
And i don't always take; sometimes i give.
I am my mother's only child,
And i am her splitting image, very wild.
Some things i've done i do deeply regret,
But most of the time it's nothing to sweat.
Let's call a spade a spade.
You wanna get laid, and i wanna get paid.

Prologue

"Oh, where...oh, where do I begin? Do I start with my pathetic daddy or my whore of a mother? It really doesn't matter where I start. It will all be a tale worth telling once I'm done.

I'm gonna start at the beginning. All I need is for you to listen to me and not judge me. So here goes..."

Chapter 1:
The Life of a Female Dog

Once upon a time, not long ago, there was a princess named Patience, who lived in a mansion, located north of Atlanta. Let me cut the bullshit. This will not be a fairytale. I wish that I could tell you a story straight out of a book. Unfortunately, I can only tell you about my lies, deceit, drama, and betrayal. Anything vindictive that you can think of, my name and picture should be next to it in the dictionary. If I could've picked my own mother, I would have done that in a heartbeat. All of my miserable life, all I knew was how to get money from men. And I learned that from the infamous Sandra, my mother. She didn't teach me much, but I observed her, and she was all about her money.

Okay. I know what you're thinking. *She couldn't have been that bad.* Well, I will be honest; she did show me how to stick a super tampon in my ass, when I first started my menstrual cycle. But that was about it. Everything else, I learned by watching her. And I mean, I didn't miss a beat.

I was enthused by everything that she had in her bedroom, like all the different fragrances that overfilled her dresser. And I can't forget about all of the dead animals she had hanging in her closet. She had furs that were handmade. She even had a few Fendi furs. I'd never heard of Elsa Schiaparelli, but Mother let it be known that her furs were a hot commodity. Also, I was always blown away by the countless rainbow-colored heels that she had in her closet. They were wall-to-wall. Mother would always say, "Old school bitches will always be better than the new school bitches."

I didn't really know what she meant, but she never let me forget it.

Daddy was around up until he made the drastic mistake of putting his hands on my mother, and that was when all hell broke loose. Mother put him out on one of the coldest winter days. And I haven't seen or heard from him since. He never called me on my birthdays, and he couldn't even be bothered to, at least, buy me a cheap-ass Barbie doll at Christmas.

So it was just Mother and me and a slew of her white male friends, who I later found out were her tricks. She had me fooled all the way up until my senior year in high school. I was in class, and my teacher Mrs. Carter, who didn't hold anything back, was talking about Bishop Don "Magic" Juan's lifestyle. I pretty much put two and two together after my teacher said that, if a woman sleeps with a man for money, she's a prostitute, and the men who pay her are known as johns or tricks. There were so many times before that I'd wanted to ask Mother if she was a prostitute, but I had been too scared, so I finally built up the nerve when I was twenty-six years old. I asked her when we were eating at a fancy restaurant in Buckhead. I remember it like it was yesterday. It was her fortieth birthday. It was just me and her, having a very intimate and private candlelit dinner. Mother had had me when she was only fourteen years old. I felt like I could tell or ask her anything, considering that she didn't give a fuck about what came out of her mouth. She never bit her tongue. But she was my mother, so I respected her no matter what. And everywhere we went, people couldn't believe that we were actually mother and daughter. I took a few sips of wine and said, "Mother, can I ask you something?"

"Sure. Go right ahead, Pee."

She had named me Patience, but often called me Pee for short.

"Are you a prostitute?"

She took a deep breath and spread her white handkerchief over her yellow velvet Gucci dress. Then, she took a sip of her expensive wine, looked me dead in my eyes, and said, "You're goddamn right! How else do you think I can afford that house that sits on five acres that we're living it up in? Hell! *Lifestyles of the Rich and Famous* ain't got shit on me. And I earned every penny that I got. I wasn't born with a silver spoon, but you can bet your pretty ass that I will die with one. And you will, too. I've dreamed of this day, and I knew that you would, one day, get suspicious and start asking questions. Listen to me, Pee, I am not going to sugarcoat shit. Ever since my mother died battered, broke, and lonely, I vowed that I would never be like her. She didn't teach me much because she was working three jobs, just to pay bills in those damn projects. Wait a minute. She did teach me how to stick a tampon in my ass. But that's neither here nor there. I swore to God that my kids would never ever see red dirt in their lives. And I'm glad I stopped having kids after you. One child was enough. Your dad reminded me of my dad, and that was why I didn't hesitate to kick his black ass out over twenty years ago. He was lazy, and I was the breadwinner. I worked with my school's work permit as an intern at a lawyer's office when I was pregnant with you. I was just a little girl with plenty of street sense. And I was going to save my money and move out of the projects. I was going to move us to where the white folks lived. I was making good money, but hell I was only fourteen, and I couldn't even rent an apartment. I could have went and signed up for a project and probably become my mother's neighbor, but who wants to live like that? I hated those damn projects. I'm glad that I didn't make any friends because those bum-ass bitches would be looking for a hand out today. Anyway, I met a wealthy middle-aged white man named Mr. Whitehead. It was his law firm that I worked at. He was very demanding, and he seemed to enjoy bossing everyone around. One day, I saw him out of the corner of my eye, looking at me.

"Now, Pee, keep in mind, I was five months pregnant with you. And all I could think of was those damn roaches that my mother and I shared room and board with. It didn't matter how much we cleaned with bleach, those damn roaches were immune to it. And I was not going to raise you in the projects. I had already prejudged him when he walked in, and I already had my mind set on what I was going to say to him if he hollered or fired off at me and treated me like the others in the office. Although he didn't look like one, how the hell did I know what a racist looked like? So, anyway, I was filing papers, minding my own business, and, sure as the sky is blue, he made his way to my desk. My heart was in my throat because I didn't know what he was going to say to me. The whole office grew quiet, and all eyes were on just the two of us. He stood there for a few seconds, watching me file papers. 'So you must be Sandra,' he said as he came closer. 'And what rock did you crawl out from under?' I stood up, belly and all, and said, 'It wasn't a white one. That's for damn sure!' He didn't say anything. He just extended his hand and said, 'I'm Mr. Whitehead. It's a pleasure to finally meet you. My daughter Cindy has told me so much about you. I love your name…Sandra,' he said.

"But, Pee, I really think that he saw something in me. Maybe he saw the pain in my eyes, or maybe he saw another single young black mother who was about to become another statistic. But he was wrong. I had money saved, and I was going to do what I had to do to live a comfortable life with you. After shaking his hand, I looked into his ocean blue eyes, and now that I think about it, back then, he was very humble, a lot younger than he is now but very humble.

"He was pissed that his daughter Cindy was always doing things her way. So, to make a long story short, he gave me his private number and told me to call him, so he could drive me home from work. I called him as soon as the clock struck five. Now, was I scared of an older white man? Yes. But fear didn't run shit in my heart. My mind told me to see what he was about, and I couldn't wait to see what he wanted with my poor black ass. When I got in his Jaguar, I was amazed at the elegance of that car. I was just a pregnant girl from the projects. I only knew about box Chevys and Oldsmobiles. I put on my seatbelt and admired the lavish car. I was quiet because I didn't know what to say. Then, he said, 'Sandra, I like how you stood up to me in front of everyone today. That's what I like, someone who has some balls.' Then, he proceeded to tell me about himself. He told me that he was a very wealthy investor who owned several businesses throughout the world. He said that he was happily divorced and looking to have a good time. Then, I interrupted him and said, 'How can a rich man like you be *looking* for anything?' 'Money isn't everything. My ex-wife got three hundred million dollars in our divorce settlement, and that selfish bitch still isn't satisfied. I could have given that slut a lot more, but what for? While I was across the map, making smart decisions and investing in some good establishments for our future, she was busy sleeping with the pool boys; she even slept with a pizza delivery boy. I should have just hired a hit man to kill her, but Cindy loves her mother dearly.'

"'You don't dress like a millionaire,' I said as I looked at his clothes. 'How is a billionaire supposed to dress?' he asked as he made a hard left at the red light. 'You're a billionaire!' I said, trying to keep my cool. 'Of course, I am. I am in the prime of my life. I am in my late twenties, and I still have my whole life ahead of me. I eat well, but I drink like a fish. And I know that you're young, but you're about to have another mouth to feed. And my offer might not be so bad. I've always fanaticized about being with a young black girl. I'm no child molester, but you are about to become a mother, and I know you could use the money.' 'Wow!' I said as I pointed him in the direction of the projects that I lived in. He saw how I was living and immediately put me in a condo in Duluth.

"So let's just say that I read between the lines, and I satisfied him. He paid my rent and paid me very good money. After I had you, he wanted to show me off to his friends. And, of course, I had to please them, too. But I didn't give a fuck. I had plenty of money, and it beat getting paper cuts and licking envelopes all day at that damn lawyer's office. They were rich white men who wanted to have a good time. I drove a 750 BMW to school. I still finished school despite all the money I was making. Although my mother didn't agree with my way of living, her tone quickly changed once she saw how much money I was giving her every week. It's just too bad that she died before I could get her out of those projects. Anyway, I made the terrible mistake of letting your woman-beating-ass daddy move in. And when he put his hands on me (you were about five years old), that was his first and last time doing that shit. He was all in agreeing with my lifestyle, but, once he saw how good Mr. Whitehead was to me, he changed all of a sudden. He wanted to drive my cars, and he wanted to pimp me out. Can you believe that shit? Mr. Whitehead had already taught me the game at an early age, so why in the hell would I listen to your daddy? I don't mean to sound cruel, but your dad and I just fucked. We weren't in love. He didn't love me, and I didn't love him. So you see, Pee, I had to suck a lot of small pink dicks to get where I'm at. After your daddy, I never let another black man touch me again. I have a wealthy bank account because I've had very wealthy clients. Do you think that a bitch with my background could afford to live in Duluth, Georgia? Take a look outside of our home, sweetheart. That grass is green, just like the money that I used to hire people to take care of it. I was blessed to come across an old trick like Mr. Whitehead, who was a billionaire. He and his friends like kinky shit, and I like green money. Now you tell me, how did it feel to drive a Porsche to school in the eighth grade? And I'm sorry that I was in France most of your school days, but I was just young, living my life, and seeing the world. But if you didn't learn anything from me, I bet you will know how to keep money in your pockets."

Chapter 2:
My Mother, My Hero

So as I continued to listen to Mother spill her heart out about her lavish past. I learned about everything, from giving a blow job all the way to having sex. It was almost like I was her therapist or something. We were so close in age that we talked about everything. And I do mean everything. We didn't hold anything back from one another. Mother's fortieth birthday was a night that I would never forget. I knew that God had blessed me with the right mother, and I wouldn't trade her for nothing in the world. But there were some things that I could probably live without knowing. For example, the way she broke life down to me. She said whatever came to mind, and she gave it to me raw and uncut. She was my hero, and, just like her, I hadn't worked a day in my life.

After that dinner, Mother still wanted to get some things off her chest. As we sat in her room, I admired her beauty and noticed that she didn't look like your ordinary prostitute. She wasn't run down like the hookers you see on the streets. Hell! She didn't even look her age. She was so beautiful to me, and I was her splitting image. We were two thick redbones. And I do mean thick. We were fit and didn't have a pinch of fat on us anywhere. Mother didn't even eat the fat off of her rib-eye steaks. My mother had class and a significant amount of sophistication in her. She didn't have to wear hair extensions, but she did anyway, and so did I. She always got what she wanted, and so did I.

I sat on her ottoman as she took off her expensive Gucci dress and put on a Natori lace chemise. It didn't matter if she was going to the corner store; Mother always had to have on some type of fashion. And she'd let people know it, too. She was very outspoken, and the fact that she had money only made matters worse. I watched her as she crawled into her plush king-sized bed.

Then, she looked at me and said, "Patience, you know I love you, right?"

"Yes, Mother. Of course, I know."

"Sweetheart, do you feel it in your heart that I love you? I mean, can you really feel it?"

"Well, Mother, I can't say that I know how that feels exactly. I mean, Mother, I do appreciate all the things that you do and have done. For example, I am blessed to be able to live in your guesthouse out back. I appreciate all the material things you've given me. But love is just so farfetched as of now. Do you get where I'm coming from, Mother? I don't want to come off sounding like a drag, but let's keep it real here. You've been out of my life eighty-five percent of the time. And look at me. I'm doing the same things that you do. Or shall I say, did. I fuck for a buck, and I do something strange for a piece of change.

"Mother, it was cool growing up with our nanny, Isabella, but she wasn't you, and I needed you. And as time went on, I learned how to cope without you. When you broke my father down to me, that was pretty much the icing on the cake. I know that you guys didn't love one another, but why bring a child into this world?"

As I talked, I saw that Mother was getting aggravated. She lit her cigarette and said, "Hold up, Patience. Do I hear a complaint about to come out of your mouth? Because if so, you can cancel that shit! I don't want to talk anymore. I've done some things for you when you were little that you don't even remember. On your fourth birthday, I hired Keana Balloons to host an extravagant birthday party. Since you're a summer baby, Keana had the perfect party theme. It was the Little Mermaid, and she knew exactly what to do. Keana decked out the whole downstairs with red, green, yellow, and blue balloons. And, in the backyard, she lined up seven kiddie pools, and you had the time of your life. I enjoyed watching you jump in and out of the swimming pool. And you were the cutest little mermaid that I'd ever seen. Keana painted your face, along with a few of our neighbors' kids faces as well. I really wish that you could remember that because you don't give me any credit.

"But I will say this, Pee. If you're looking for an apology, you will never get one. I made sure you went to the best schools, wore the best designer clothes, and drove the best cars to school. I've always wanted for you to have only the best things that money can buy. And what about all of those expensive-ass hairstyles you were getting every week from Vicki at OV's on Glenwood in Decatur? I know you remember Vicki because you used to practically beg me to let you get those snatched-back ponytails."

"I remember her," I said as I had a flashback of the things that Mother didn't let me do.

She never would let me go to the Golden Glide skating rink. There were times when I would be getting styled in Vicki's chair and hear those other girls rant about how much fun it was to go to that skating rink. They made it seem like they always had the time of their lives. All I wanted to do was be in a crowd with girls my age and my color. But that only happened when I went to school. And even then, those uppity, snobby white girls weren't on my level. Everyone at my school was rich and preppy. The only reason I fell into their category was because Mother had money. Sometimes, I wished that my grandma hadn't died. I would have loved to live in the projects with her. I bet it would've been fun to live that life and grow up and then be about that life.

I quickly erased those project memories and looked over at Mother. She was daydreaming. I asked, "Do I see tears rolling down your rosy cheeks, Mother?"

"Yes, I'm reminiscing about Omar. That boy knew he could do some hair. And when he passed away, it hurt me to my heart. God bless the dead.

"I remember the first time I met him. He had such a happy spirit to me, and, whenever I saw him, he'd always have a smile on his face. I met him through Nikki, and she's another soul that left us too early. Do you remember Sylvia? She was Nikki's best friend. They were together all the time. I sometimes teased them by calling them Ebony and Ivory. Those two definitely had each other's backs. Sylvia really took Nikki's passing to heart. Sylvia was also on two television shows, fighting back tears while being interviewed about Nikki's death.

"Hell, we all took Nikki's passing to heart and the way she died was just plain unimaginable. Nikki used to lay Sylvia's hair to a T, too. Vicki didn't have nothing but talent working at her shop. And some of their work was so good that they were featured in local and national hair magazines.

When Vicki and her crew went to the Bronner Brothers Hair Show, they definitely got the respect that they deserved. She had people coming from near and far to get their hair done. Her hair salon was always filled to capacity. Do you remember when we got there at noon and didn't leave until five in the morning? Those were some good mother/daughter moments that I can reminisce and laugh about."

"I always had to sit in a chair and wait, while you got your hair done. You consider that quality time?"

"Can I get some credit for that? Even though we spent hours in there getting our hair done, we kind of bonded a little, don't you think? I enjoyed listening to Mrs. Bailey talk about the good old days. And that Keta, Vicki's cousin, she brought life to my hair every time she laid hands on my head. It was worth the wait. She had me looking like Anita Baker at times, but a light-skinned version, though."

I saw through Mother, and I had to interrupt her because she was starting to make it be all about her. I mean, really, how does she expect a four-year-old to remember a birthday party? I looked at her and said, "That's just it, Mother. We never talk about anything that is of importance. All we ever talk about is white dicks, expensive clothes, and money. I never had a childhood because I wanted to be like you so bad. You didn't even get mad when Isabella called you in Paris to tell you that I'd dropped out of school. It was actually dumb on my part to get all the way to the door and quit. I was a senior when I found out about you and your white friends. Mother, that really messed my mind up for a minute. But then I shook it off because the reality was that I wanted to do what you did. I wanted the fast money. I wanted the fast cars. I wanted to be catered to at five-star restaurants. I wanted to do everything that I'd seen you do. Mother, you had me thinking that you were giving all those men massages, but you were selling your body for money."

"Good money!" she screamed as she flicked the ashes into the ashtray from her cigarette. "Listen to me, Pee. I don't have to explain a damn thing to you. Sweetheart, life isn't fair, but you have to roll with the punches or get punched. I never sold you to men, and that's something you should be proud of me for. Your life could have turned out worse. I could have given you up for adoption, but I didn't. I loved you enough to keep your ass. And now twenty years later, you want to question me about my lifestyle? I mean, come on, Pee. I'm not the world's greatest mom, but I'm not the worst either. I got turned out at the tender age of nineteen. And you started selling your body at seventeen. And that was your prerogative! I wasn't mad when I got the phone call from Isabella that you'd dropped out of school. Hell! I'm surprised it wasn't sooner than that. You have always had everything handed to you. You could have easily lived off the money that I was giving you. You didn't have to sell your body like I did. So, when you came to me and said that you wanted to be a high-class whore, I didn't try and stop you because your johns would be my johns. And that meant I wouldn't have to worry about any harm being brought to you. And they were very good clients, I might add. Sweetheart, I probably don't know how to express my love for you wholeheartedly, but I did know exactly what you needed. I made sure that you were taken care of, and I do know that you don't need love in this world when you got money. I can go anywhere in these beautiful United States and get treated like a queen, and do you know why? Because I have money. And when you have money, you're a 'somebody.' But when you're dead broke, you're a 'nobody.' I don't regret anything that I've done. I'm only playing the hand that I was dealt in this life. I was destined to raise you in the best neighborhood. I didn't want you to experience poverty. Period! Point blank!"

"But, Mother, what about all the things that I witnessed as a child?"

"Patience, if you don't change the subject, it's going to get real ugly in here real quick. You mean to tell me that now this shit is starting to get to you? Sweetheart, you're in your twenties. You can get out. You can go to college. You chose to do this. And I'll tell you right now. I'm never stopping this. The money's too damn good."

"But, Mother, wouldn't you like to get married and maybe even have another child? I mean, you're only forty years old. Don't you want to be happy?"

"Sweetheart, look around you. We are living the life...a damn good life, I might add. We don't have to worry about shit. Nothing!"

"Well, Mother, I want to get married one day to a black man," I said as I raised an eyebrow. "I want to have kids one day, but I don't want to expose them to different dicks and shit."

"If I were you, sweetheart, I'd enjoy life and not bring a child into this world."

That statement alone let me further know that Mother didn't give a damn about me.

Chapter 3:
Who Needs Logic?

I knew the way that Mother and I were living was so ungodly. But, when you're a child and accustomed to things, such as money, good food, and good booze, what's a child to do? I wanted the best things in life, too. As time went on, Mother and I would bypass each other near the pathway that separated the guesthouse from her house. Even though the castle's stone steps appeared to be never ending, I saw her johns, and she saw mine. "That's just how the cookie crumbles," and that was Mother's favorite saying. That was her answer to almost anything in life. It was like she almost expected the worst. But, for the life of me, I could never understand Mother. She was so forthcoming and very outspoken. I once asked her, "Why don't we ever attend church?"

She said, "That's how the cookie crumbles, I guess. My mother never exposed me to God."

Then, I asked, "Do you believe in God?"

She said, "I believe in God. I believe that the Creator gave all of us life. The main thing I believe in is money and only money. I don't believe in coincidences or fate because I didn't luck up on the things I have in life. I worked hard for my money. And I don't believe that money is the root to all evil. In fact, money is the root to all happiness. I love being the center of attention when I flaunt my valuables out on the scene. I enjoy walking into five-star restaurants with all eyes on me. I always light up a room as I walk in slowly, as if I were a model walking on the runway. Then, I always do a slight turn and eye the room to see if I see anyone that I know. And it's always possible because I frequent the same restaurants and clubs as my johns. I've even run into a few married ones out with their wives. But don't think men are the only ones running around and doing dirt. Women are dogs, too."

And I had to agree with her because we did the same shit. But my life wasn't any better. I just knew that I had it all figured out, until one day the unimaginable happened. One of the johns wanted me to shit on him. It didn't matter that he was paying five grand—I just couldn't seem to do it. I couldn't picture it, let alone get in a position to defecate on his chest. Mother had warned me that there were some strange characters out here. I wondered if she'd ever been asked to do something like that. I wondered if that was included in her "that's how the cookie crumbles" phrase. Mother had often told me that there would be times that I would likely almost never reject any money. But, this time, she was wrong, I couldn't even stomach that thought. Tom was his name, and he so furious when I told him no. He stormed out and went to Mother's house. They both came back, and I was looking at Mother like she couldn't be serious. She ordered Tom to lie down on the floor. Then, she untied her robe, stood over him, and shitted on him. I was blown away. He had his dick in his hand, jacking it as her shit seeped out of her ass onto his chest. He even wiped her ass and got pleasure from it. I watched him as he was moaning and sweating like he was about to jump out of an airplane and skydive. The cum that shot out of his dick almost reached the top of the ceiling. When it was all over, there was a white man lying on my floor with his chest covered in shit, and Mother collecting the five grand.

"Now, Pee, that's how you shit on a motherfucker. Go in there and shower, Tom," Mother ordered as she thumbed through the crisp one hundred dollar bills Tom had given her.

"Yes, ma'am," he said as he got up, stumbling a bit.

I was disgusted, and it didn't seem to bother Mother one bit. I watched him as he carried the comforter to the bathroom to clean up. I couldn't register what had just happened because I had just witnessed my mother shitting on somebody.

And it had all happened so fast. She looked at me and said, "Sweetheart, it comes with the territory. Pee, there are all kinds of nuts out here, and, if you want to last in this business, you have to get with the program. It took me five minutes to make five grand. You can't be scared, girl. This is our life, and we have to do this."

Tom flew past us both, saying, "Thanks, Ms. Sandra."

"Wait a minute," I quickly said. "Where is that shitty-ass comforter?" He turned around and got it from the bathroom. Then, he looked at me and said, "I won't be needing your services ever again," before slamming the door behind him.

That was the last that I saw of Tom. Mother let out a loud laugh as if something was funny. So apparently, she was used to this type of shit.

"Oh, sweetheart, don't worry about him. He'll be back. They always come back. They love our sweet black pussies. They can't get enough of us. We're one hell of a mother/daughter duo."

From that day forward, I was cold and numb to the world. It was a cold, cold world, but I was colder. I didn't let anything stop me from doing or getting what I wanted. I was a trained to-go whore, and the world had to be ready for me. After seeing the many outrageous things that Mother did, I'd do the same and put my own spin to it. Mother looked me in my eyes and said, "Sweetheart, I am only a few feet away. Don't hesitate to call me when you come across another john like Tom."

Chapter 4:
Whores Need Love, Too

When I think about my life, I don't want to elaborate on it specifically. Although I was a high-paid whore, I wanted to be different from Mother in a sense. I wanted to get married and have kids. I knew it seemed a bit much coming from me, but that was what I wanted in life. But Mother made it clear that I should never have kids. She told me that she was too young to be a grandmother. She said that kids today were crazy and that they were killing their grandparents off. And some had even killed their own parents. She said that she would not be on the local news because her grandchild had killed her. I thought it was absurd for her to even be thinking of anything like that. She said that she didn't trust anyone, and she didn't put anything past anyone. She said all she trusted was herself and money. She loved money, and it showed. Her garage was filled with different cars that I couldn't pronounce.

One day, when Mother and I didn't have any johns lined up. I went to Mother's house. Since the door was always unlocked, I walked in and found her relaxing in the family room, watching television. She looked at me and said, "See. This is why I don't want grandkids."

She was watching a crime show, and the headline was about a young teenager who had murdered her grandmother. But neither one of us were violent, so how could a child of mine be violent? But if Mother didn't want any grandkids, I wouldn't give her any. I sat there, watching the show with my mouth wide open, because I couldn't believe some of the stuff that I was hearing and seeing.

"There are some sick people in this world," Mother said. She turned the television off and said, "So what brings you by here, sweetheart?"

"If you want, I can wait to tell you since you're still in awe of killer grandkids?"

"No, go ahead, Pee. What do you have to tell me?"

I took a deep breath and said, "I'm in love."

She chuckled and said, "Whores don't fall in love."

I said, "Well, this whore named Patience is in love, and I want you to meet him."

The next thing that came out of Mother's mouth without hesitation was, "Is he black or white?"

I said, "You'll see."

She said, "Pee, you know that I don't like surprises."

I said, "You won't be surprised, Mother."

"So where did you meet this man?" she asked as she stared me dead in my face.

"I met him at the Tavern. It's a restaurant that has some very good food, but they are famous for their chicken wings. It's just south of here."

When I said *south*, Mother's eyes grew big. It was almost like she had started having flashbacks of her own childhood. "What do you mean, south of here?"

"I mean, I wanted to see something else in Georgia, other than the north part."

"But, sweetheart, this is home, and the south isn't where you belong."

"Mother, can I just finish telling you my story please?"

"Continue," she said with rage in her voice.

"So, anyway, I was listening to the radio, and I heard that this place called the Tavern at J.R. Crickets has karaoke. And it's located on Tara Boulevard. They also have other locations at Camp Creek, Campbellton Road, and Stonewall Tell. The ad also mentioned that they have good crab legs and Two Dollar Tuesdays. Mother, I just wanted to go someplace where I could just be myself. You've seen how we're looked at when we enter those five-star restaurants. Those people look at us like we don't belong. Mother, for once, I wanted to go to a place where I could let my hair down…you know, just relax and not be judged by the public's wandering eyes.

"So I went to the Tavern, and I was greeted by the owners Russell and Ronnie Cotton. They are two black brothers who I think that you would find very attractive."

"I don't do black men, but go on," she said.

"They look almost like twins, but Russell is darker than Ronnie. They are both kind, and I can tell that they are good people. Even though Ronnie seems to be the mean one, he is actually a nice man; he just doesn't smile very much. And that's because he is all about his business. He makes sure that his establishment is nice, clean, and family friendly. Russell, on the other hand, is very flirty and friendly. Mr. Russell has some spark in him. The staff is very professional, and the atmosphere is right up my alley. Black People," I said, letting her know that I enjoyed seeing them because all I knew was white this and white that. Maybe Mother should have been born white. I often wondered, *If she was born white, would she want to be black?*

"I entered the Tavern, and Mr. Russell seated me at a table. As I sat there, looking over the menu, a young lady approached me. Her name was Antoinette Smith. I had watched her go from table to table, but I didn't know what she was doing. I wasn't really paying her any attention. She had on a Straight to the Point Books T-shirt and the pants to match. She was damn near out of breath by the time she got to my table, but I made out what she was saying. She said, 'Hi, I'm Antoinette. Would you like to check out my books?' 'These are books?' I said as I reached for them. I thought that these were movies or something. She said, 'Movies? Nah. These are my books, and you can relate to any one of them.' As I looked at the colorful covers one by one, she gave me descriptions about each one. She had written a total of five books. Her first book was called *Daddy's Favorite Pop*, and her second book was called *Married, Sneaky Black Woman*, and her third book was called *White Cop, Lil Black Gurl*. Her fourth book was called *I'm a Drag, Not a Fag*, and her fifth book was called *Black-Out on Bankhead*. She also said that she was working on her sixth book called *Women are Dogs, Too*. I kind of smirked when she said that because all I could think about was you and me. We are the prime example that women are dogs, too. I listened to her, and I ended up buying all five, and I must say, they are some jaw-dropping tales, especially *Daddy's Favorite Pop*. She said that that one was based on a true story, and it literally had me in tears. She even showed me an interview on her iPhone. She had been a guest on the Frank and Wanda Morning Show on V-103. The interview was filmed, and the episode aired on Channel 69. She was a very cool person, and I want you to meet her, too."

" Look, Pee, get to the point. Who is this woman? We don't need any orphans in our lives."

"Mother, she's not an orphan. She's just a girl who's been through a lot, and she expresses her pain on paper. She said that she was molested by five of her uncles. They would smile in her face every day, and then be under her covers at night. And even though they had women of their own, they still preyed upon her young body. She said that she had developed breasts at an early age, and she thinks that that was one of the reasons why those men did what they did.

"Mother, do you know that she's never been loved and that she doesn't know how to love? She said she has five kids who are the Five Lights of her life. Mother, then our conversation got even deeper; she used to sell her body, too. Of course, she wasn't getting big money like you and me, but she has a lot in common with us."

"Okay. I will meet your friend Antoinette," she eagerly said. "Now, get on to this Romeo you seemed to have met."

"As Antoinette and I were talking, a man came to our table and vouched for her books. He said that her books were very good, a bit graphic, but he told me that she was definitely the number one street author in Atlanta. She ended our talk and told me that she appreciated me patronizing her and that she had enjoyed our conversation. We've talked on the phone, and we've become very good friends since then. Then, the man said, 'You won't be sorry that you bought them books. What's your name anyway?' He took a seat at my table. 'I'm Patience,' I said as I noticed his Crest smile. 'I'm Dee,' he said as he signaled for a waiter to come to our table. 'How are you guys doing today?' the waiter asked us. Then, the waiter looked at me and said, 'I've never seen you in here before.' He extended his hand and said, 'I'm Mr. Russell, the owner of this joint.' I said, 'I'm Patience, and, yes, this is my first time here. I heard of this place on the radio station.' 'So what can I get for you two?' Mr. Russell asked. Dee ordered a double shot of Grey Goose with a splash of cranberry juice. I was still looking over the menu and didn't have a clue what I wanted to drink. I didn't see any liquor that I was familiar with. Then, Mr. Russell said, 'I will fix something special just for you since this is your first time here.' Mr. Russell came back with a tall glass that was blue and frozen, and I saw the liquor on top. I could tell that it was a strong drink, and I was used to strong drinks. 'Here you go,' he said. 'This is called the Mr. Russell. I hope you like it, and I hope you guys enjoy the rest of your day.' I took a sip of the drink and looked at the stranger who had just welcomed himself at my table. 'So where are you from? I've never seen you around here before,' he said as he checked my ring finger out. 'Again, my name is Patience, and, no, I'm not married. And I'm definitely not from around here.

"Then, he said quickly, 'Well, you should be married. You look like the type that I could wife. I feel like I already know you.' He stirred the cranberry juice in his cup. I had to ask him where he was from because he was the one with a thick accent. He was from Tennessee. And although he had some gray hair, he wasn't old at all. He was very attractive to me. His teeth were perfect, and his nails were clean. We talked for a good while, and we have been dating ever since that day. So, Mother, I want you to meet him, but I don't want him to come here. I don't want him to see this big house."

"Hold the fuck up, Pee. My lifestyle has nothing to do with him at all."

"Dee and I had lots of fun together. He took me to Lenox Mall and Phipps Plaza. We ate good at Houston's. I even tasted his salmon, and you know I don't like salmon. When it was all over and done, he made me feel so special. He made me feel loved. Mother, he's the reason why I want out of this lifestyle. He showed me that there is so much more to life than what I'm doing."

Mother didn't take the news of meeting Dee very well, so she never met him. Mother told me that I was living in a fantasy world, and it wasn't love at all. It was lust.

Chapter 5:
Owner of a Lonely Heart

Mother and I were two miserable souls, and it didn't matter how much money we had. At the end of the day, we were lonely, tired, and shameful. At least, I was shameful. Mother made prostitution look like taking candy from a baby. She surrounded herself with material things and self-medicated. She never wanted to face reality, and the reality was I was just like her. She didn't feel guilty for exposing me to her hellish lifestyle. She didn't feel guilty for telling me how to keep a dick wet when I sucked it. She was like the mother of the devil. She didn't hold back anything. It didn't matter if I was young with tender ears. She wanted me to be a thoroughbred, just like her. She wanted me to have tough skin just like her, too. But there was a soft side to me, and maybe I got that from my daddy. I never recalled Mother and me having any heated arguments because what she said usually went.

I don't recall her having many friends. And asking about family members was out of the question. Ever since I was a little girl, Mother made it very clear that it was me and her against the world. I remember going to school, and, every morning, while Mother was combing my hair, she'd remind me that we had to always look out for each other. And her ways were deep down in my soul. Mother and I did the same shit every day like clockwork. But I was missing two main things out of my heart, and they were love and a man. When I was with those johns, some made me feel like the Queen of England. And then there were some who made me wish that I was never born. It was my choice, and I could have stopped, but it was something about tricking that I couldn't let go of. Some days, I would love to be eye candy for those johns and be seen just about everywhere with them. Then, there were days when I found myself balled up in a hot shower, crying at the shit I'd done. I was lonely, and I needed love, real love. But all I was getting was lust and money. I never felt good about what I was doing. But when I did do it, it didn't matter. Because it was almost like it came natural.

I had already perfected and mastered the craft of tricking. Even when I did it for the very first time, I was happier than the trick. I never thought I would lose my virginity this way, but that's how the cookie crumbles. I'd always pictured myself having sex for the first time with somebody who was my age. But that didn't happen. My first time was with a john who had a foot and ankle fetish. He didn't want to have sex right off. He wanted me sit in the middle of the bed, Indian-style. Then, he got naked and opened my legs. He grabbed my feet and rubbed them on his dick, and his body jerked as if he was having an orgasm. But that wasn't the sick part; the sick part was he wanted me to kick him in his balls as hard as I could. And, of course, I did it because I was frustrated about a lot of shit. I had no problem kicking him with all of my might. He turned red in the face, but he took it like a man. After he came to, he laid in the bed and continued to rub my feet across his dick. I thought for sure that he wouldn't want to have sex after that, but, boy, was I wrong. He wanted to fuck me in my ass. He didn't have a big dick which didn't make it too bad, but it was very uncomfortable. Those days were so crazy for me.

I told Mother about that sexual encounter, and she had an answer for everything. She told me that I should have got on top of him. That way, I could have propped his dick up against my clit and rode back and forth. She said he would have never known the difference. Mother was so nonchalant about everything. It didn't matter what the situation was, if she didn't care about something, she would tell me straight up.

One time, I was on my way out to meet Antoinette at the Blue Flame. Mother saw the clothes that I was wearing and said that I looked like Raggedy Ann.

"I'm going to a strip club, and Antoinette said that I could wear whatever I want."

Mother looked at me and said, "No daughter of mine will go outdoors looking like that. Sweetheart, I don't care if you're going to a roach motel. You should always look like a million bucks, even if you don't have a single coin in your pocket."

Chapter 6:
Living Life in the Money Lane

I had left Mother without warning. I gave up on trying to have a relationship with her. There was no talking to her. Even with tears in my eyes, she never gave in. I'd never seen Mother cry. The only time I'd ever seen her shed tears was when someone died. I mean, I felt like she never had any love or compassion for me. She was always on top and in control of every aspect in her life. She always kept a smile on her face. And she was always a woman of her word. If she said she would do something, she did it. If she wanted something, she got it. I left all Mother had to offer and went on a hunt for love, but the things that I came across weren't fulfilling. I wanted a man who could take me away from the world. I wanted to live in a bubble. So finally I met the man of my dreams. His name was Tiberius. I met him at a fast food joint. He was smelling good and definitely looking handsome in his work uniform. His complexion was like that of the outside of a walnut. His eyes lit up his face, and they were brown in the sun. The moles that were under his eyes were in the exact same spots. He had a temp fade, and it was lined up to perfection. He looked so sexy to me. He was the perfect man; his body was in perfect shape. His arms were not too big. They were just right for his size. And I wanted to be with a black man, considering that Mother hadn't been with one since my daddy.

I moved west of Atlanta, to the Vinings area. Tiberius and I moved very quickly. We didn't waste any time having sex on the first night we met. We were both feeling our alcohol, and my pillow-topped queen-sized bed was in for a treat. We talked, and then we fucked. It was that simple.

I was well on my way to having the perfect life. Tiberius was a hard-working electrician. He was the only child, and I was, too. That was what made us so perfect for each other. My house wasn't too fancy, and it certainly would have not been up to Mother's standards. But I was happy with it and so was Tiberius. He let his loft go downtown and moved in with me. We moved in together after knowing each other for only eight months. Some things were very challenging for me, but I didn't want to go back and live with Mother, so I managed to get along with him very well. I didn't tell him anything about my past because my past was my business. But I was curious to know about his ex-girlfriends. And he was upfront with me and told me that he was just a man looking for love, too. And that some of the girls that he had come in contact with were only using him for his money. I thought to myself, *That is too bad for those bitches because he is all mine.* And he put the dick down in the bedroom. It was big and pretty, just how I like my dicks.

I felt his pain and that made me want to love him even more — even though I knew, deep down inside, I couldn't love anyone, not even myself, but it was fun pretending that I was in love with him. He made me feel like a princess. He rubbed my feet and complimented me every day of the week. I thought that was so sweet. I enjoyed playing the role of a wife. I cooked, cleaned, and had his hot bubble bath ready when he got off work. We watched movies, and we had great sex. This was the first time that I actually enjoyed having sex. I experienced real orgasms with Tiberius. He really took the time to get to know my body. He knew exactly what I needed, and he knew exactly how to give it to me. I didn't have any complaints, but the whore in me was starting to come out. It didn't matter that I had a good man at home. It didn't matter that he licked my pussy until it was dry. I wanted some outside dick. And I could hear Mother's voice in my head saying, "Every woman in the world has done something strange to drive a Range." And the thing about my mother was that she was always right. No matter what I did, I have always thought of her watching me. When

I would order my food, I could hear her voice in my head saying, "Get plenty of lemons in your water." She always said that lemon water was very good for our hygiene. She would say, "Don't no man want to smell a smelly ass pussy." Mother had a remedy and a saying for just about everything. If I said that I had a headache, she'd say, "You need some dick." Everything with her was always about dick and money. And little did Tiberius know the Sandra in me was slowly coming out.

Chapter 7:
I Know What Boys Like

For the first couple of months, our relationship was just fine. We did everything together. I mean, wherever you saw Tiberius, you'd see me. We were joined at the hip. I knew I was dead-ass wrong for my actions. My best friend Sunflower had warned me to stay away from married men. I'd often confide in her and tell her that I was sleeping around with them. But she didn't know the real me. She and I became friends when I was a junior in high school. She was a very nice friend, but she had no idea that I'd been a prostitute since our senior year. Some things are just not other people's business. I had been with plenty of married men before. I mean, of course, they were all white. And I wanted to be a one-man woman. But it was almost like dick was calling me in my sleep. I didn't know what was wrong with me. I was pleased with Tiberius's big pretty dick. But I wanted more; I wanted to be in character with him almost every night. So I tried dressing up. I had dressed as everything, from a maid all the way to being a hooker, which I totally was. Tiberius was pleased at first, but I think that it bored him. Sometimes, he'd go along with my sick head games. Then, he'd become very quiet, and I could tell that the more I acted out, the more distant he became. I didn't say anything; I just carried on like it didn't bother me.

One morning, while I was out for a jog, I met Cornelius. As I stretched on the curb to get warmed up. I saw him, and he sure was something nice to look at as dawn broke. He was dark brown, and I saw the waves in the top of his head from a distance. He was bringing his trash can to the bottom of the hill. And before I knew it, I had opened my big mouth and flirted.

"Hey," I said.

"Hey to you," he said.

"I'm Patience. I live three houses up." Then, I looked at his arms and thought, *My legs would look good on top of them.*

His teeth were pearly white, and his thick lips looked bitable. Then, he said, "I used to run around the block, too, to stay in shape because I was in the Air Force, but, since my wife took ill, I retired, so I could be here for her and help with my little ones."

"Oh, I'm sorry to hear that. What's wrong with your wife?" I asked as if I was interested. I could care less about another bitch. The only thing I was interested in was his dick inside of me. As he talked, I pictured myself sucking his dick in the middle of the street. I pictured myself whipping his dick out of his sweat pants, teasing it with both of my nipples. Then, I'd slurp up and down on it as he pulled my hair, while looking into my eyes. My pussy was getting wet just thinking of that. Then, I snapped back to reality, and I heard him say that his wife had ovarian cancer.

"You look too young to be married," I said as I stretched, bringing my leg up to my chest. So he could see my fat pussy print in the tight workout gear that I was wearing.

"I am young, if you consider twenty-eight to be young."

"You're twenty-eight?" I said in disbelief. "You look younger than that. And what on earth possessed you to get married?"

"It was the right thing to do I guess you could say," he said as he grabbed the morning newspaper. "I got my high school sweetheart pregnant, so I made her my wife. The same thing happened to my parents. My father married my mother when she became pregnant with me."

"But do you love her? I mean, why do people get married because of a child when they don't even love one another? Do you love her, or are you in love with her? There's a difference, you know?"

He scratched the top of his head. "You might be right. I'll have to think about that," he said as he headed up his driveway.

"Where are you going in such a hurry? I'm not finished talking to you," I said, not realizing that I was following him up his driveway.

"What's with you?" he said as he turned to walk backward, and proceeded to look at his front door.

"Well, I will tell you if you stop walking." Then, I said, "Tell me your name again." I hadn't forgotten his name. I had a memory like an elephant. I wanted to stare into his eyes a minute more.

"My name is Cornelius. You don't remember? I told you already. But you can call me Cee."

"Cornelius, huh? I like that name. Well, my name is Patience, and I also have a nickname. It's Pee. So where is your wife right now?"

"She's in the house, resting. She's bedridden because she's always in constant pain."

"Bedridden, huh?"

"Yes, I have to wait on her hand and foot."

"So it sounds to me like you need to relieve some stress."

"I think I need a vacation, but that's impossible because I have to watch my kids."

"You mentioned your parents. How come they can't watch them for you?"

"It's really not that simple. My parents are up in age, and they are just too old to watch them."

"How old are your kids?"

"Devin is nine, and Sinai is seventeen."

"Those kids are old enough to watch themselves."

"You sure are asking a lot of questions about me. What's your deal?"

"I don't have a deal. I just do whatever I want to do. And right now I would love to suck and fuck you. Have you ever had a woman come on to you?"

"Yes, plenty, but I've never really entertained them because of my obligation to my wife Cherry."

"Cherry, huh? That's a pretty name," I said, thinking of my next move.

Then, he said, "I can't believe you just said that."

"You better believe it because I am very direct. When was the last time you had sex or got your dick sucked?" I knew that, since his wife was bedridden, I had plenty of time to ask him whatever I needed to know.

"I've never cheated on my wife, and it's been a long time since I had sex. I mean, I get my rocks off by watching porn and jacking my dick."

"That sounds fine and dandy, but it's nothing like real, sloppy, wet, good pussy," I whispered as I grabbed his dick at the same time.

"Cut that out," he said as he looked to see if any of our neighbors were watching.

"I told you I do what I want to do. Let's go in your garage so that I can give you a sneak peek."

"You are all kinds of crazy," he said as he proceeded toward his front door.

"I'm serious."

He cracked a smile, and I could tell that he was enjoying my freaky conversation.

"Let me show you what I can do."

"You don't even know me," he said as if he was thinking about taking me up on my offer.

"That's the beauty of it. I don't need to know you. I only need to know your dick."

Chapter 8:
Fuck Me. Feed Me Dick

I could tell that he didn't take me seriously. But I was dead-ass serious. I had to show him because actions speak louder than words. I knew that I had to take control of the situation because, if it was up to him, we would have been debating about fucking for hours. I grabbed his hand and led him into their two-car garage.

"This sofa is perfect," I said as I forcibly threw him onto it.

He didn't do anything but let me take control and have my way with him. I manhandled him. I was turned on by his curly eyelashes. I was turned on by the moles that were lined up along the left side of his neck. He looked as if he was in shocked, but the more I wrestled with getting his big, hard dick out of his pants, the more comfortable he became. I kneeled down and assumed the position and was about to put his dick in my mouth. Then, he said, "I've never, in a million years, had this happen to me. All I was doing was taking the herby curby to the bottom of the street. And here you come out of nowhere."

"I don't see you trying to stop me," I said as I put the head of his dick in my mouth. He grabbed my head and slowly eased the shaft of his dick into my mouth. He was moving slow with the rhythm of my head. Then, I switched up and deep throated his dick and twirled my tongue around the head of his dick. I knew that he was enjoying every minute of it. I could tell by the way his toes curled up in his Nike slippers. His dick was dark, thick, and hard, and I took my precious time slurping up and down. I was enjoying it, too. My pussy was hot and wet, and I was ready for him to fuck me as soon as I finished deep throating his hard dick. I wanted him to remember every minute of this moment.

"You like that?" I asked as I stroked his dick up and down with my hand. He just looked at me, then quickly looked at the door to the entrance to his house. "It's not even eight yet," I said as I looked and noticed him biting his bottom lip.

"I have to get my kids ready for school. The bus will be here shortly."

"Well, do you want me to stop or continue?" I asked as I licked up and down his dick.

"Can you please stop? But I want you to stay. It'll only take me fifteen minutes to get them ready. I'll be right back," he said as he eased his dick out of my mouth. It was still hard as a rock as he fiddled with and put it in his pants. As he walked away, I noticed that he walked with his head kind of tilted to the side. He had a one of a kind walk, and I would know that walk from anywhere. It was kind of sexy to me. I loved watching him walk away. He was every bit of six feet tall. And I loved his dark brown complexion. When he closed the door, I got up and looked around his garage. He had so many different Nike tennis shoes. I mean, there was, at least, one hundred pair or more. Then, I walked over to the other side toward the door to the inside of the house. I cracked the door open to peek in and saw that they had very nice furniture. *What am I doing?* I thought. I know for sure that if I did get caught that his wife couldn't beat my ass. His house was similar to mine, except his stairs to go upstairs were near the front door. I opened the door all the way and closed it back quietly.

"Hmmm…that must be his wife," I said as I glanced at a family portrait that was on the wall. "She's pretty but not as pretty as me." I walked through their entire downstairs. "Nice taste," I said as I flopped down on the soft lime green leather sofa. "What's this?" I said as I walked over to a vase that was on the fireplace mantel. When I picked it up, I heard footsteps, so I tried to sit it back down, but it fell, hitting the floor. I ran into the kitchen.

"Dad, what was that?" I heard one of his kids say. I peeped around the corner and saw Cornelius and his kids heading to the front door.

"It's nothing, sweetheart. Have a great day in school." He walked over to the vase, shaking his head. "How the hell did this happen?" he said as he kneeled down to pick it up.

I looked closer, and they were ashes. *Damn! Did I just knock over a dead person's ashes?* I watched him as he just stood there, puzzled. He headed for the stairs, and so did I. I tiptoed to the bedroom that he went into. I took my shoes off and put them behind the door. I couldn't believe that he didn't hear me or come to see if I was still in the garage. His bedroom was so huge. He had a big king-sized bed on one side. On the other side was a hospital bed that his wife was in, but I didn't expect to see what I had seen. The room had been transformed into a hospital room. There were different machines beeping with colorful lights on them. Then, I saw his wife, and she was hooked up to so many machines.

"You won't believe what just happened," he said as he grabbed an IV bag. "Kevin's ashes fell on the floor. I think I have a pretty good idea how they got there."

I looked over at his wife. She didn't move, nor did she awake. He was talking to himself. Or maybe she could hear but couldn't respond due to all of the heavy medicine she was on. He grabbed a small bottle and inserted its contents into the IV bag.

"There, sweetheart. This should make you feel a little better. This morphine should do the trick."

"Shit," I said as I bit my finger. "Those were really ashes!"

As he headed for the door, I jumped out and said, "There you are."

He was startled and said, "What are you doing in my house? Are you crazy?"

"No, I'm not crazy. Let's finish what we started in the garage."

"I can't register what's taking place right now," he said as he walked past me.

"Daddy, all you have to do is lie down on that king-size bed over there."

"Do you not see my wife over there in the other bed?"

"Yes, I see your wife in the other bed, but your wife can't see us."

"Do you realize that you knocked over my child's ashes?"

"Oh! About that. I'm very sorry."

"You should have just stayed in the garage. I was coming right back."

"So I see that one of your kids passed, and I'm so sorry to hear that."

"Yes. Kevin was Devin's twin. He lived longer than the doctors had expected him to. He was born with a hole in his heart and passed from those complications at the age of six."

"Oh, poor baby, you have so much to deal with. Your son died, and now you have a vegetable for a wife. Wait. Did I just say that out loud? I'll tell you what. Why don't we head over to the other bed, which I can clearly see is yours? You need to relieve some stress, and it looks like I hit on the right man. I'll make you feel good. Sorry about calling your wife a vegetable."

"Don't be sorry," he said.

"She's on hospice. We all agreed that her last days would be here with us."

I grabbed his hand and led him to his bed.

"Now, where were we?" I said as I took off my shirt and threw it on the floor.

"First, I have to go get up Kevin's ashes."

"I promise. Once we're done, I'll get the ashes up myself," I said as I took off my pants. I couldn't believe how I was taking total control. With the johns, I was always being told what to do.

I got on top of him and looked into his dreamy eyes. I saw nothing but hurt and pain. His eyelashes were so long and curly. And the sunlight from the window made his brown eyes light up. I grabbed him by his face and kissed him. It was the most romantic kiss that I'd ever had. Tiberius and I had never even kissed like that before. He grabbed my neck and kissed me harder. He looked into my eyes and made me feel like I was the most beautiful girl in the world. Then, I felt something in his mouth. I stopped kissing him, looked at him, and said, "What is that in your mouth?"

"Oh! These are my retainers."

"But your teeth are already perfect."

He sat them on the side of the bed, and we began to kiss again. His lips were so soft, and I felt his hard dick as it pressed against my stomach. Neither one of us thought about a condom. I knew that he wanted to feel some real pussy, considering his situation. I looked him in his eyes and said, "Are you ready for this?"

He raised me up, and I slid his dick inside of me. I was riding him, kissing him, biting his bottom lip. It felt so good. I was moaning, and, each time I rode his dick, I came all the way up, letting his big, thick dick come all the way out and go all the way back in. I was riding it fast then slow, and then I'd stop and squeeze my pussy muscles, gripping his dick. He was grabbing the lower part of my back and slapping my ass. The harder I rode him, the harder we kissed. I was so mesmerized by his eyes. I could ride his dick all day. I was definitely feeling him. Then, he flipped me over and slow stroked his dick inside of me. I felt like I was in heaven.

"I'm about to come," he said as he fucked me faster.

"No, don't come just yet," I whispered.

"But, baby, it's coming, and I can't help it. Your pussy is so good; I can make love to you all day."

"Make love to me?" I said.

"Yes, that's what I'm doing now. I'm looking into your big, beautiful eyes, and this is the best feeling in the world to me right now. Your pussy is wet, tight, and just right. Plus, I haven't been with a woman in years."

"Well, let it go, baby. Just let it flow," I said as I nibbled on his ear.

"Ooh, baby. Here it comes." He jumped up just in time because I didn't want his nut in or on me. As soon as I was about to reach for my shirt, we both looked at each other when we heard his wife's machine go beep.

Chapter 9:
No Crying, Just Moaning

"Oh, my God!" he said as he jumped up. "I think she just died!"

"Wait! Let me clean you up first."

He said, "Never mind that," and he put on his pants. I put on my clothes, too. We both walked over to her side of the room slowly. "I am not ready for this," he said as he grabbed my hand.

I looked at her, and she was just lying there. And the machine was still beeping as if she'd flat lined. Then, she started to moan. I watched her chest as it rose up and down. Her moan was like a gremlin after it had eaten after midnight. I was frozen, and, as I got closer to her, I looked at her nails and saw that they were so long. There was a scarf wrapped around her head.

"She's not dead," he said as he felt her head. "You really should be going."

"I've been here with you this long. I don't mind."

"I mean, I don't want you to see her like this."

"We just had amazing sex less than five minutes ago. And now you want me to leave?"

"All I'm saying is that maybe I'm confused."

"Oh, baby. That's okay. I understand," I said as I rubbed my hand across his chest. "There are some things that happen in life that we have no control over. You are supposed to feel exactly the way you are feeling because you are indeed going through a great deal of pain. If I was in your shoes, I don't know what I'd do. But I'm glad I met you this morning. Now I feel like I've known you my whole life."

"Excuse me...Dad, I forgot my lunch money." We both looked spooked as his seventeen- year-old daughter Sinai walked into the bedroom. "And who is she?" she asked, looking at me with an attitude.

"Oh, this is your mother's new nurse," he nervously said as he looked at me. Then, he bumped me and said, "Tell her who you are."

Then, she looked at me again and said, "If you're my mom's new nurse, then why you don't have on any scrubs? And where's that thing that goes around your neck so that you can listen to my mother's heartbeat?"

"You mean a stethoscope?" I said as if I was really a nurse.

"Yeah, that thing," she snapped.

"Well, I have the perfect answer for you. I was on my way to the gym, and I got an emergency call from your dad. Your mother was low on morphine, and I just happened to be in the area. I had some in my car, and I dropped it off."

"But I didn't see your car outside, and why are you still here if you just needed to drop it off?"

This little bitch was giving me the third degree. I wanted to say, "I'm the bitch that just fucked the hell out of your daddy," but I didn't. I changed my tone and decided to use some reverse psychology on her.

"What's your name, young lady? You sure are feisty and pretty, too, I might add."

"I'm Sinai."

"What's your name?" she asked me with her hand on her hip. "You don't have on a name tag or anything. Some nurse you are."

"Well, like I stated earlier, I was on my way to the gym. And my name isn't important. I am a nurse."

"Here. Come and get your lunch money," Cornelius said as he went over to the dresser. "You can finish," he said as he nodded toward his wife, indicating for me to go to her bedside. I couldn't believe he really had me in character. It was kind of fun because that was what I did with my johns. I loved to pretend and be something that I was not. I knew he couldn't let his daughter know that he'd just been fucking someone in the same room as her mother.

"Are you scared of her or something? She's dead. She can't hurt you," I heard Sinai say. "What did I tell you about saying that about your mother?"

"Well, she is dead; all she ever does is just moan in that bed all day. I'm sick of it, Daddy. Why won't you just pull the plug and cremate her like Kevin?"

"Listen to me, sweetheart. Your mother still has vitals. She still has a heartbeat. She's heavily sedated because the pain is unbearable. That's why she moans all day." I looked over at Cornelius as he was trying his best to explain to Sinai. I wanted to kick her in her ass. She had such a smart-ass mouth. I could tell that she was waiting for her mother to die. She wasn't crying or sad. All she wanted was her damn lunch money.

"Well, everything looks normal," I said as I lifted his wife's eyelids. Her pupils were fixed and dilated, so Sinai was almost right. She wasn't dead, but she was very close to the end. I felt her hands, and they were cold and purple. "I must be going now," I said as I headed for the door.

"No. Stay. What's the rush?" Sinai said. "My dad always has the nurses over for hours at a time." She was starting to get under my skin. And I had it in me to slap the taste out of her mouth. I couldn't believe that she said that he had nurses over here for hours. *Did he lie to me?* I wondered. Maybe he was waiting for her to die, too. I didn't know what to think. All I wanted was some dick. And it seemed like I had run into a funeral home with a teenager from hell.

"It was nice meeting you," she said to me with a smirk on her face. I didn't say anything. I only gave her a hand gesture. She left, and I turned to him and said, "So how many nurses have you fucked?"

"I don't know why she said that. Sinai is a troubled teen, and she says things that aren't true sometimes. She's taking this thing with her mother very hard. My wife has been in this state for almost a year now."

I believed him because I didn't like his daughter one bit. I wanted to feel sorry for her, but Mother had always taught me to never feel sorry for the next bitch.

Chapter 10:
Not Everybody Has a Conscience

When it was all over and done, I stood there for a moment longer, looking into his eyes. They say that you can "realize lies through the eyes," but I was mesmerized by his light brown eyes, and I didn't give a damn if he'd slept with every nurse at Grady Memorial Hospital. As long as I got to fuck him when I wanted to, I would be fine.

"So what's next?" he said as he turned the sound of his wife's machine down.

"What do you mean? I'm going to do as I promised and get your son's ashes up. Again, I'm so sorry."

We both went downstairs, and I went to the pantry to get the broom and dust pan.

"I can do that, you know?" he said.

"No, I got it. A deal is a deal."

He took a seat on the sofa and watched me as I got the ashes up.

"Where do you want me to put them since the vase is broken?"

He gave me a mixing bowl, and I put them in there.

"I feel bad, and I'm very sorry for snooping around and barging in here on you like that."

"Yeah, tell me about it. You have some nerve."

"That wasn't a punch line for you to jump in and agree with. It was said for you to simply listen. Can I ask you a personal question?" I said as I sat beside him on the sofa.

"Sure. Go right ahead."

"This may come off as me being mean or a bitch. And you can answer it however you like. Hell, you can even kick me out. But my question to you is, why haven't you pulled the plug on your wife yet? I mean, she can't cook for you, and she sure as hell can't fuck you. She can't do anything for you. And that moan would give me nightmares. Geesh! She sounds like an elephant in labor. But I have to give it to you. You're a strong man. If I had a husband and he was in that situation, he wouldn't have even left the hospital. He would have died in the hospital. That's where people are supposed to die. And you have your dying wife on her deathbed in your bedroom."

"Are you done?" he asked as he sat up on the sofa, looking a bit uncomfortable.

"Am I offending you? I'm just merely speaking my mind."

"No, you're not offending me. I thought I made it clear to you that her last wish was to spend her last days here at home with us. I don't have a problem with her moaning. The cancer is eating her insides. You have no idea what type of pain she's in."

"That's my point exactly. Why don't you just put her out of her misery like they do horses that are injured in a horse race?"

"It's not that easy. I took vows. I married her. I still love her. I'm in love with her."

"Well, you weren't in love with her when I had your dick in my mouth. And that was less than an hour ago. You weren't in love with her when I was riding the hell out of that pretty black-ass dick. You weren't in love with her when—"

"I get it," he said as he cut me off. "What's your deal? You are definitely a one of a kind chick. And I have never in my life ever met anyone like you. Why are you so nonchalant about this whole ordeal? Do you have any type of compassion in your heart?"

"As a matter of fact, I do. I have compassion for dick. I have compassion for sex. I have compassion for money. And if you want me to, I'll pull the plug for you because I can tell that this is killing you. This is where the vow 'till death do us part' comes in at. It's time for her to die."

"Can you please stop mentioning the word *die*?"

"Is *deceased* a better word to use then?"

I could tell that I was pissing him off. I backed off a little because he had some good-ass sex, and I wanted to keep getting it, but I could not have sex while that wife of his was in a coma with that ridiculous-ass moan. I had it in me to get rid of her ass once and for all.

As we continued to sit on the sofa, we both became quiet. He was probably thinking about his wife, while I was thinking about another fuck. I was picturing him bending me over on the sofa as I faced the patio. I pictured him fucking me hard from the back and doing it as fast as he could. I got off the sofa, walked behind him, and began to massage his neck.

Then, I thought about the lie that Mother had told me about her massaging all of those men. I stared off into space and didn't realize how hard I was massaging his neck and shoulders. I felt him moving as if I was, in fact, hurting him. I slowed up my pace and massaged him more tenderly.

Often times, when I had flashbacks of Mother, they always seemed to depress me, and it sometimes made me go into a state of mind where I just didn't give a fuck. I mean, there were times when I was sucking Tiberius's dick and a memory of Mother would come in my head. And I would get pissed off at him and physically bite his dick. I mean, bite down on it when it was rock hard in my mouth. I think that was why he sort of became distant from me. I really believe that he wanted to leave me, but he was too scared to go anywhere. He thought that I was crazy because I had never wanted him to meet Mother and didn't talk a lot about family like he did. He knew that I had a couple of screws loose. And, to be honest, I think that he really felt sorry for me. I thought that was why he wouldn't leave me yet.

"That feels so good," Cornelius said.

After he said that, I kissed him on his ear, reached down in his pants, and rubbed on his hard dick. His pure body scent smelled like coconut as I licked his neck, taking long, wet strokes. Then, I whispered in his ear, "Are you ready for round two? We can have sex right here on the sofa."

"Not in front of Kevin's ashes," he said as he jumped up and quickly removed the ashes.

I didn't say anything about the ashes because I didn't want to ruin the mood. My pussy was hot and ready, and I was ready to feel him inside of me again.

"Sure. Please put them away," I said as I eased out of my clothes. It didn't matter to me if his soul was in the room watching us. I just didn't care about certain shit. I could tell that he loved to kiss, and I didn't mind. His tongue was so warm, and his kisses felt just right. He hugged me with passion, and I felt good in his arms. He laid me on the sofa and sucked my pretty toes. It felt so good coming from him, considering the physical attraction I had toward him. I looked down at his curly salt and pepper hair. The more he tickled my toes with his tongue, the more my pussy got wet.

Chapter 11:
Meddling

Well, I suppose that times flies when you're having fun, but time was definitely on my side today. I went to my house and grabbed some clothes to change into. Tiberius was still at work. When I walked in the house, I turned all the lights off. Tiberius was bad about leaving the lights on. I grabbed a few of my sex toys. The Platinum Jack Rabbit was, by far, my favorite. But I brought a few more with me, just in case, like the silver bullet and the Orgasm in a Box.

Cornelius was a confused soul. I could tell that right off the bat. I mean, he had just let a stranger barge into his house. He had no idea who I was, but, hell, I didn't know who he was either; he could have been a lunatic, too. I definitely know that I have a couple of screws loose, but I loved the chemistry that we had. And I'd only known him for a few hours. There was something about his eyes. There was something about his voice. There was something about that walk of his. He was my type of guy, and that was for sure.

When I got back to Cornelius's house, I took a shower in his bedroom as he attended to his wife. I even cooked us brunch. The aloe vera juice that he had was very chilled with a bittersweet taste. I didn't like the taste of it, but I'd had worse shit in my mouth before, like unwanted dicks.

We sat at his kitchen table and ate the meal I'd prepared. The tender steak strips were cooked medium, and the seasoned red potatoes and onions were good to go.

"I hope you like this," I said as I sat the plate in front of him.

"It looks and smells good," he said as he grabbed the steak sauce. "I can't remember the last time I had a cooked meal. Would you like to say grace?" he said, looking at me.

I closed my eyes and thought, *I've never said grace before.* When Mother and I would sit down and eat, she'd only give thanks to her money. I playfully but seriously said, "No, you go ahead and say it."

As he put his head down and began to pray, I looked at his thick lips as he gave thanks to God for the food we were about to eat. *He is all kinds of cute,* I thought.

"Amen," I said as I smiled at him. Then, I switched gears, asking him about his outspoken teenage daughter. "So why haven't you had a cooked meal in a long time? I know that daughter of yours should, at least, cook you a hot meal. I mean, you are her daddy after all."

"Well, technically, I'm her step-daddy."

"Step-daddy? Really."

That's even better, I thought. *Maybe, once his wife keels on over and dies, I can get rid of her little smart ass, too.* There was something about her that I didn't like. And I sure as hell didn't like her questioning me like I was one of her peers. I didn't like the way she looked me up and down either. I knew I was gonna have it out with her. *She will respect me and talk to me like she has some sense.* Then, he looked over at me and said, "I will start off by saying that she's not taking the news too well that her mother will be dying soon. I can only imagine what she's going through. I mean, I'm doing my best with her, but, as a step-dad, there is only so much that I can do. You know as a man and all. She respects me up to a certain level. I mean, she goes to school, and she gets good grades half of the time. But she ignores curfew time. She sometimes makes it in on time, but then there are other times when she stays out the entire weekend."

"Have you tried finding her real daddy?" I interrupted. "Because girls at that age really need their dads in their lives. Trust me, I know."

"The last thing we heard about her real daddy was that he is doing hard time in prison. And speaking of life, tell me about yours."

I almost choked on my potatoes. I had no idea that he was even interested in me other than for sex. I didn't know where to start, nor did I know what to say. Then, I cleared my throat and said, "Well, for starters, I'm your neighbor. I live three houses down, and, oh, yeah, my zodiac sign is a Gemini. And I do a lot of Gemini shit. Do you believe in astrology?" I asked, trying to change the subject about me. "What's your sign? Wait. Let me guess. You're a Virgo, nah…you act more like a Libra, but I'm sensing you may be a Scorpio, by the way you put it down in the bedroom. Then again, I may be wrong. You may be a Capricorn, a loyal lover. But only in the bedroom, though."

Then, he looked at me and said, "What are you? A sex astrologist?"

"You can say that since I am a very good judge of character. I study the signs. Then, I ask people what sign they are. Then, they turn out and do or act just like their zodiac sign says. So tell me, what is your sign?"

"Well, you're kind of right about me. I'm a Capricorn, and I used to be loyal in everything. I was a loyal father. I was a loyal husband. I was a loyal step-dad. And then life hit me in the face like a bag of bricks. I have to watch my wife deteriorate right in front of my eyes. I lost one of my sons. And now I have to listen to my step-daughter disrespect me, like she has never had any type of home training whatsoever."

I saw that he was about to break down, and I'd never seen a man cry, and he was beginning to tear up. I wanted to jump on his dick again, but I knew that pussy wasn't the answer to all his problems.

Chapter 12:
Men Cry, Too

I didn't know what else to say or do to him. I gave him my deepest sympathy, but my feeling sorry for him wouldn't save his dying wife or bring his son back. He went on and on, talking about his life. He, soon, balled up like a baby and cried like one, too. I held him as the tears continued to roll down his face. *This is a job for his mother. My job is to satisfy men sexually*, I thought as I held onto him tighter. I felt as if I was going to drop a tear or two, but my numbness wouldn't let me do it. There was just something odd about me when it came to feelings. And I knew I had gotten that from Sandra Denise Washington, my mother. I had to thank her for just about everything that had happened in my life. I mean, from the money that I made all the way to my nonchalant-ass attitude that I had copped from her. Mother has always said that that's just the way the cookie crumbles. I wanted to tell that to Cornelius, but he didn't need to hear Mother's twisted-ass nursery rhymes.

"Is there anything I can do for you?" I asked as I looked him in his eyes, wiping his endless tears away.

"You've already done enough," he said as he held my hand tighter. "I wish that things were different. I wish that it was me who was lying in there on that bed, instead of my wife. I wish it was me who had died instead of my son."

"Come on now, Cornelius. You can't beat yourself up and start playing the blame game. I don't know much about God, but I do know that God does exist. And I also know that he is in control of everything all the time."

"I believe in God with all of my heart, too," he said as he got up to get a few paper towels to dry his face. Then, he walked over to their entertainment center and showed me a CD with a cute light-skinned man on the front cover. "Do you know who this is?" he asked as he handed me the CD.

"I sure don't," I said as I read a few tracks from the back.

"That is James Fortune and FIYA, and he is an incredible gospel composer. I listen to his song called 'Live Through It' every single day. I'm not gay or anything, but his voice is anointed, and he was born to sing. His voice touches my soul, and I cry every time I listen to his music. The way he talks to his choir as they blow them songs makes me feel like I can make it through anything. I love all of his songs, but there is another song on there, and it's called 'I

Trust You.' His music really uplifts me, and I need to listen to it now more than ever. I also look at him on YouTube, and he is definitely a gospel sensation."

As I looked at the CD track list, I noticed a song on there called "Identity," and I thought, *I would give anything to change my identity.*

He was in a zone, talking about gospel songs, and I had my mind in the gutter as usual. Then, he took the CD from me and put it back on the entertainment center. He looked at me and said, "I know you're not going to believe this, but I was raised in the church. I was taught to do everything perfect. My parents told me to marry my first girlfriend. They said, 'No sex before marriage.' They told me that my dick would fall off if I had sex before marriage."

"Whoa! Whoa! Wait a minute! You mean to tell me that your wife is the only piece of pussy you've had all your life? You never cheated with one of those overseas women? You mean to tell me you never even got your dick sucked by someone over there? It's no wonder that you didn't stop me and all of my sexual advances. You wanted to fuck me just as bad as I wanted to fuck you. You're no church boy...raised in the church, my ass. You're just as naughty as I am."

He smiled, and I was glad that I was able to put a smile on his face. "I can't believe that I just spilled my heart and soul out to you. I don't even know you, and here I am crying to you."

"It's okay. You didn't know me when you had your dick in my mouth earlier either."

We both chuckled. I looked at my watch and knew I had to call it a day with him and go home to Tiberius.

"I must be going," I said. "We won't be needing these," I mumbled under my breath as I grabbed my bag of sex toys.

Before I left, he grabbed me and kissed me, asking when he would see me again. "I feel like I've known you my whole life," he said as he kissed me once more.

I teased and said, "That's a side effect of me, considering you've only ever had one piece of ass in your entire life."

"You got jokes, I see," he said as he walked me to his front door.

"All I'm saying is, I can't believe that you've only had sex with one person."

"Well, that is normal, you know? That is what people do when they're in love with one another. I mean, real true love. I do love my wife deeply, but this situation has taken a toll on me, and I don't know if I'm coming or going."

"Well, if you stick with me, you'll keep coming," I joked.

"There you go with the jokes again. I'm serious," he said without a smirk or smile on his face. "How about you tell me what's going on in that pretty head of yours?"

"Who me? You don't want to hear nothing about my boring life. I feel like I'm a housewife without the title. My boyfriend Tiberius used to be exciting, but now all he does is keep himself busy with work. I know there isn't that damn many sockets that need to be fixed… or whatever the hell it is that an electrician does."

"It sounds like you got yourself a good man, too."

"If I had a good man, do you think I'd be here at your house fucking and sucking you like there's no tomorrow? Not to mention, I'm doing it in front of your dying wife."

"Whoa! Whoa! Whoa!" he said with a frown on his face. "That's enough."

"I'm sorry," I said as I grabbed the doorknob to open the door. "I didn't mean to sound snobbish, I think I just had a slight flashback of my own fucked up life."

"I accept your apology," he said as he kissed me one last time.

The door flew wide open, and it was Sinai. She'd seen us kissing and said, "Let me guess. You're my dad's new therapist."

Chapter 13:
Young and Dumb

"So am I right? You're Dad's new therapist, too," Sinai said as she barged her way in between us.

"Sweetheart, it's not what it looks like," Cornelius said. Then, he looked at me for confirmation. I had it in my heart to slap the piss out of her.

"It is what it looks like! I saw you kissing this strange lady…I mean, Patience. At first, you said that she was my mother's new nurse. And then I walk in *our* home, and she's still here, looking like she's been getting fucked by you all day! Did you forget that my mother is upstairs dying? You couldn't even wait until she took her last breath!"

I couldn't believe that this young, dumb-ass bitch was reading me. I heard her correctly the first time, but I was still shaken that she had called me a *strange lady*, even though she knew my name.

"Wait a minute! How do you know my name?" I said as I snapped my neck at her.

She bucked her eyes and rolled her neck, snapping her fingers, saying, "That isn't important. Just know that I am not as young and dumb as you two think I am. The fact still remains that I walked in on you two kissing. So, Daddy, what do you have to say for yourself? You seem to have an answer for everything else! I'm waiting for an explanation."

"First of all, I need for you to calm down."

"I am calm!" she screamed. "Now, tell me, why were you kissing her?" Then, she looked me up and down as if I had an infectious disease. I held my composure because I was seconds away from slapping her.

"Sweetheart, there is no explanation. This lady is just being nice and helping me with your mother. That was a friendly kiss that you saw."

"Oh, my goodness! Will you please cut out the bullshit? She's no damn nurse! I'm not stupid, and I know what I saw." Then, she kissed her hand and said, "This is a friendly kiss, a peck or a smack. I saw you two swapping spit. Her tongue was in your mouth! And your tongue was in her mouth. And look at her hair—"

I cut her off and said, "I'll tell you exactly why I'm here. Are you ready for my answer?"

"No!" Cornelius said as he shoved me out the door.

"She doesn't have to leave. I'll leave," Sinai said as she hurried past us, running out the door.

"Wait! Don't go," Cornelius said, but it was too late. She took off running like a track star. "All of this is wrong," Cornelius said as he pounded himself upside his head. "I wasn't raised like this. I know better. This is not what God wants me to do."

"Please don't start that crying shit again. I'm still pissed at her. She talked about me as if I wasn't standing here."

"She has a lot on her mind, okay?"

"No, it's not okay, and she's going to have a lot in her ass, like my foot." I was pissed off because that little bitch had the nerve to say that I looked like I'd been getting fucked all day. My blood was boiling, and I wanted to ride through the projects and pay a couple of girls to kick her ass for me. If I touched her, I would get put under the jail because I would do more than beat her ass; I'd probably kill her.

"Look. Things are just crazy and haywire around here. There have been a lot of things going on here lately," Cornelius said.

"Well, why don't you just pull the damn plug?" I knew I was out of line, but what was the use of his wife if she just moaned in pain and agony.

"It's not that easy. The doctor said that she only has a few days left. I'm just carrying out her final wishes."

I raised my voice and said, "News flash! People die every day. As a matter of fact, someone just died right now. Right as we speak, someone in the world has just taken their last breath. And someone will die ten minutes from now. My point to you is that your wife is suffering, and you seem to keep calling on God and bringing him up. What do you think God thinks of you for letting your wife continue to suffer? You need to put her out of her misery, have a nice funeral, and move on with your life. I've never seen anything like this, not even on Lifetime."

"If I pull the plug, will you attend the funeral with me?"

Chapter 14:
Murder or Set Free

He was dead serious, and he had definitely called my bluff. But I couldn't back down now.

"Hell, yeah! I'll pull the plug and sit right by your side at the funeral. I can see that you don't have the heart to do it. It's all starting to make sense to me now. She's your first love, and you can't do anything to save her. I am really starting to relate and understand why you feel the way you do."

"Do you really?" he asked as his eyes began to water.

"Yes, I do."

"Because, for a minute, I was starting to think that you had no emotions at all."

"I have emotions, but they're not for shit like this. And that's another story that I do not care to talk about at this time. Now, let's go back here and pull this plug," I said as I grabbed his hand. We both walked slowly down the hallway to the stairs.

I was talking tough, but I didn't want to pull a plug. I just wanted her to go away. It was so awkward for me to have these feelings for him so quickly, knowing she still existed. The closer we got to their bedroom, the faster my heart began to skip beats in my chest. When we walked in, we saw that she had no movement. None whatsoever. I mean, her chest wasn't even rising up and down with the help of the breathing machine. The machine wasn't even beeping. Then, he ran over to her and said, "She's dead!" He hugged her with tears rolling down his face, saying, "It's over now. Thank you, Jesus. Her pain is finally gone. Sweetheart, there's no more pain and suffering." He was rocking back and forth with her in his arms. He cried out loud to God, saying, "Thank you again, Jesus, for taking her." Then, he fell down to his knees, saying, "Father God, please forgive me for I have sinned against your will."

I watched him embrace and show love for his wife, and I was relieved, too, because I didn't want to pull no damn plug. Then, I saw out the corner of my eyes that smart-ass Sinai was back and so was her little brother.

"Dad, is she dead?" I heard his son ask.

"Yes, son. Mommy's gone to Heaven with your brother Kevin."

"Can I go?" he asked as he began to cry.

"No. Come here, son. How was school today?"

Sinai walked over to her mother, looked at me, and said, "You killed my mother, didn't you, bitch? You'll be sorry that you ever stepped foot into this house."

"Are you threatening me?" I said as I got into her face.

"No, I'm not threatening you. I'm making you a promise."

Cornelius got in between us and said, "Sinai, she had nothing to do with this. It was the work of God."

She didn't want to hear nothing that he was saying. She covered her ears and walked over to her mother. Then, the tears started to roll down her face. She didn't say anything. She just stood over her mother. She rubbed her face, and then she held her hand. She bent down and whispered something in her mother's ear. Then, she kissed her mother on her forehead and her lips. After I watched her be a freak show to her mother, I saw that she turned her attention and focus on me. I had actually calmed down from her smart remarks from earlier. But seeing her all over again had pissed me off even more. *And then she really thinks that I killed her mother. And she had the nerve to threaten me. This little bitch doesn't even have a clue about me. She obviously does not know who my mother is.* I thought something else was definitely up with this girl. I would say that she reminded me of me. But I didn't wear knockoffs. I never did. She may have had a spunky attitude like me, but that was about it. And all teenagers today, especially the ones who ran over their stepfathers at a time like this, definitely had more than daddy issues.

Then, Cornelius looked at her and said, "Sinai, I can't deal with you and your attitude right now."

"You don't have to deal with me. As a matter of fact, you don't have to see me ever again in your life!" Then, she looked at me and said, "Don't forget the promise that I made you, bitch," before she stormed out.

She did it again, I thought. *She looked at me with a straight evil face and read me like I was one of her friends.* I looked over at Cornelius and saw that he was holding his son. They were both crying. *This is definitely my cue to leave*, I thought as I looked over at his wife. She was already starting to turn blue in the face.

I said, "Are you going to call the coroner or the police or somebody? You've called on God so many times today, and he definitely answered your prayers."

"Can you call them for me?" he said while handing me the phone.

I called the police department, and they were there in no time. As I looked at his son, I felt a little sorry for him. He'd just lost his mom, but I didn't feel sorry for his sister.

That bitch deserved to hurt for the way she had been talking to me.

"Sir, we'll take it from here," the friendly paramedic said.

Chapter 15:
Missing Links

I left Cornelius and told him that I would come back and help him with his wife's funeral arrangements. I had to gather my own thoughts and get myself together. And, for the life of me, I was going to get a piece of his daughter. She had no idea who she was fucking with. As I walked along the sidewalk, I noticed a van across the street that read MR. GOOD DECK HOME IMPROVEMENT. *I wonder whose house needs improvement*, I thought as I unlocked my door. When I walked in, it was exactly how I had left it. There was not a light left on, and the television wasn't on either.

"He hasn't been here," I said as I sat at the foot of our bed. "Hmmm...that's strange."

I called him on his cellular phone, and it went straight to his voicemail. I didn't know any of his friend's phone numbers to check to see if he was with one of them. I knew his mother's phone number, but she didn't like me, and I didn't like her. Her exact words were that "we are moving too fast." She wanted to meet my mother, but I told her that my folks were dead, so that shut her up from ever asking me about anyone in my family again. As I looked around, I began to see Cornelius's wife's face everywhere. I saw her in the corner. I saw her on the wall. And, to make matters worse, I heard that horrible moan. I went to the medicine cabinet and downed six white capsules. I didn't even know what type of pills they were; I had to have something to calm my nerves. The voices in my head wouldn't stop, and I couldn't get them to stop either. There was no way I was going to sleep in this house alone. Then, I heard very loud voices, and it was his wife screaming at me, saying, "You killed me! Are you happy now? The plug is finally pulled."

"I didn't kill you, bitch! God took you!"

Then I thought, *Why am I talking to a dead bitch? I'm not scared of anyone but Sandra!* I locked my house up and walked back to Cornelius's house. As I walked down the sidewalk, I thought about what his step-daughter had said to me. She promised me that I'd be sorry for ever stepping foot in their house. *She has some fucking nerve. Who does she think she is? I can do whatever I want. I'm about to leave my mark all over their house.*

Then, I heard someone say, "That's the way the cookie crumbles."

"What the fuck?" I said as I looked around to see if I saw anyone. But that voice sounded too real and too familiar. Could it be Sandra? Did she follow me to see my new life? I rang the doorbell, and Cornelius came to the door wrapped in a thick black robe. His initials were embroidered on it.

"Come on in," he said as he locked the door behind me. Then, he looked at me and said, "Sinai finally apologized. And she said she would apologize to you, too, but not now. She wants to apologize to you on her own terms."

"Are you serious? She really wants to apologize to me?"

"Of course, I'm serious."

"But she seemed so adamant about the words that she swore out of her mouth. That little heifer actually threatened me."

"Sweetheart, let's just forget about her for now," he said as we headed to his bedroom. "What a day," he said as he flopped down in the recliner. "Can my life be any more of a disaster?" he cried out.

"It actually could," I said as I looked at his wedding picture on the dresser. "You should thank God that you have more options in your life. If I were you, I'd look at this as a favor from God. Now, you can go out and have yourself a ball and not feel guilty about it. I still can't believe that you have been fucking the same old stale pussy."

"I was just doing the right thing. I mean, I have morals and values that I do value, unlike some people in the world."

"Why are you saying that like I don't value anything in my life?" I said with an attitude. "I value things, too."

"What do you value?"

"I value money, my car, my expensive weave, my expensive clothes, and this voluptuous ass of mine."

Then, he said, "Those are all material things. The things you just mentioned aren't of value at all. Well, maybe the car…hypothetically speaking. But, since you've been here, all you've talked about is death and money. When I say 'things that are of value,' I mean, your character, your heart, and your regard for another human being's life. A woman without moral values is like a lost needle in a haystack."

"Well, aren't we the judge of character all of a sudden?" I said as I stretched out on his bed. "It almost seems as though you got some balls now that your wife is dead." When I said the word *dead*, he looked at me with a serious look on his face.

Then, he said, "Now is not the time for your sarcasm."

"For my what?" I said as I twirled my hair.

"Nevermind," he said. "Can you give me a hand with this bed?" He was about to fold up the bed that his wife had just died on.

"Sure. Why not? And good riddance to it."

"Let's put all of her things in the garage."

"How about we put all her things at the bottom of the street?" I said as I strained to lift one side of the bed.

"Look!" He said as he rubbed his temples. "Her things are sentimental to me."

I could tell that he was losing his patience with me, but I didn't care. I had a plan, and my plan was to have him all to myself. Then, I paused for a minute and said, "You're right. I do have a heart. I just don't use it as much. I understand. You're absolutely right. You should keep all of your wife's belongings."

As we were taking the fold-up bed to the garage, we heard the doorbell ring, followed by a loud beating on the door. We both went to the door, and it was the step-daughter from hell.

"Where is your key?" Cornelius said as he opened the door for Sinai to walk in.

She looked at him and said, "You have no right to ask me anything. My only parent that really cared for me is dead." Then, she looked at me and said, "Why are you still here?"

Cornelius motioned his hand in front of me so that I wouldn't snap or do anything to harm to her. But I wanted to beat the living hell out of her.

"Sinai sweetheart, it doesn't matter how you look at things right now. I'm still your daddy."

"You're not my daddy. You're my step-daddy, and don't you forget it!"

"Why are you so hostile all of a sudden?" he asked.

She continued to stand there, looking at the floor, ignoring everything that came out his mouth.

I thought, *What in the hell kind of family have I stumbled upon?* I looked at her, in her eyes, and saw that she was filled with hate. And so was I. I really wanted to do some harm to her. At that moment, my thought process was like that of Sandra's. She didn't care what she did to people. So why should I? I had so much of her in me that I couldn't even pretend to be myself. And that was just it. I didn't even know who I was. I was just a cold-blooded bitch, and I don't care about nothing or nobody but myself. So, as I stood there, I had to listen to his smart-ass step-daughter, without being able to strangle her or punch her in the face.

"Do you hear me, Cornelius?" she said to him as if she was the parent. "You do not have the right to ask me anything!"

I was in a daze, thinking about Sandra, and then I heard Sinai say, "I want to speak at my mother's funeral."

"Sweetheart, that's not a problem," he said as he went for a hug.

"DO NOT TOUCH ME!" she said as she headed up to her bedroom.

Chapter 16:
I Don't Hate. I Masturbate.

"You don't have to always go after her, you know?" I said as I followed behind him as he went after Sinai.

"Yes, I do. I feel as though she's going to hate me for the rest of her life."

"Well, then, so be it! Let her hate you because I'm starting to hate her ass."

"She's a child, and you're the adult. Why don't you act as such?"

"I am acting as such."

"Well, I'm showing her that I am concerned about her feelings, as well as her well-being.
She is still my daughter, no matter what. I don't care if I am her step-daddy. I've been in her life ever since she was three years old."

When we walked into her room, Sinai was shoving clothes into an overnight bag.

"Where do you think you're going, young lady?"

"I won't be here as long as you have her here," she said as she looked in my direction.

"Do you mind stepping out for a second?" he asked me.

I wanted to do some stepping all right, but I wanted it to be on Sinai's face. "Sure. I'll step out and go to my house for a little while."

"How about you go and stay there until you die?" Sinai blurted out.

"I'm warning you, little girl. This is not what you want," I said as I backed out of her room slowly. I couldn't believe that this girl had it in for me. I was not the reason that her mom had passed away. Hell! All I'd wanted was some dick from her step-daddy. I will find out what's really going on with her and why she acts like she really hates me.

As I walked into my house, I noticed that the lights were on and that I must've just missed Tiberius because I smelled the aroma of his Jay Z's Gold cologne lingering in the air. I wondered what his deal was. I hadn't heard from him since he'd left for work earlier that morning. So I picked up the phone once again and tried to reach him on his cell phone.

"Still no answer," I said as I looked around the room.

Hmmm...his clothes were still in the closet. Well, I could tell that he still didn't have the balls to pack up and leave me. Despite all I did, he stayed. My life with him was an arrangement. I think he felt as though he had to stay with me. We thought it was love at first sight, but it had turned out to be lust on the first night. I quickly became bored with him, and he got tired of my ways — period. I thought it was all the alcohol that I'd consumed that had me head over hills for him on the first date. He was very affectionate, and, at first, I couldn't get enough of his kisses. Then, all of a sudden, the thrill was gone. After putting the thoughts of Tiberius out my head, I decided not to go back to the house of hell. I thought it would be best if I let Cornelius and his wicked step-daughter work things out by themselves. Those two were indeed a mess and a disaster waiting to happen. I ran a hot bubble bath, and I put on some slow music. I lit a lot of scented candles to set the mood. *Tiberius might come back home tonight and make passionate love to me. He is also a man full of mystery. Like now, I'm really wondering where he disappeared to.* I stood in front of my tall mirror and began to take my clothes off slowly as if I was auditioning for a role in porn. I danced to the music from the bedroom to the bathroom. I placed one foot in the tub. *Whoa! That's too hot for me.*

I ran a tad bit more cold water, and, as soon as it was fit for me to get in, I went all the way under. The water felt so good that it almost felt like I was washing my guilt away. Then, I grabbed the baby oil and poured it on my dark brown nipples. Those men loved my breasts, and I could see why. They were so firm and perky. I often licked them whenever I was riding a john. That drove them crazy.

My breasts were so perfect that I didn't have to wear a brassiere, and, when I walked, they both jiggled and all eyes were on me. And I loved it when those men licked both of my breasts at the same time, too. That really made my pussy flow wet like a river. As soon as the baby oil reached my nipples, my pussy became hot like an oven. I rubbed both of my nipples at the same time, making my pussy wetter than it already was. Then, I grabbed the Jelly Water Vibrator. I turned it on full speed and placed it against my nipples, letting it tickle them. I felt like I was about to come just from the sensation on my breasts. I slid the vibrator down my stomach and moved it in a circular motion on my fat clit. I liked to make my orgasm last, so I played with it inside of my pussy to the beat of the music. Then, I licked my juicy lips, imagining that I had Cornelius's dick in my mouth. His dick was big, black, thick, and tasty. The more I thought about him, the faster I moved the vibrator in my pussy. The temperature of the water and the baby oil mixed in with the water was a great combination. I moaned Cornelius's name as I felt myself about to come. Then, I slowed up my pace because I wasn't ready to bust just yet. I was in total control of my body, and my mind followed because having an orgasm is a mind thing. I could come quickly in a millisecond, or I could make it last for almost thirty minutes like I was doing now. I giggled to myself, and I started to talk out loud, pretending as if Cornelius was in the tub with me.

"Yes, baby, put that chocolate dick in my mouth. Fuck my mouth! Fuck my mouth harder!"

I turned over in the tub and rode the vibrator like I was riding a real dick. I was splashing water everywhere, and I was almost at my peak. I laid back in the tub again and placed the vibrator on my swollen clit. Then, I started to scream Cornelius's name again. "Yes, Cornelius baby, fill my mouth up with your hot delicious sperm." I moaned his name, and, as I came on the vibrator, I imagined that he was coming in my mouth at the same time and that I had swallowed it all, without spilling a drip.

Chapter 17:
Dazed and Confused

After making myself come several more times before going to bed, I walked to the end of my driveway and looked down at Cornelius's house. I wondered if he had gotten anywhere with Sinai. She was trouble. He didn't see it, but I did. I saw right through her and the games that she played. She was the type of girl that tested one's patience. But I would always be ten steps ahead of her as long as I continued to wrap Cornelius around my finger. I hopped on my queen-sized bed with its colorful oversized pillows. I threw some on the floor. Then, I grabbed one and put it between my legs, and dozed off to sleep, wishing it was Cornelius.

###

I woke up the next morning, feeling good and refreshed. I checked my phone and still had no call from Tiberius. There were only calls and voice messages from Mother. I decided to call Mother back just to see what she wanted with me. I thought that, since I'd just upped and left, she had gotten the picture that I didn't want to emulate her lifestyle anymore. I called Mother.

She said, "I want you to come home. I don't understand why you left all of a sudden. I love you and miss you."

As she was talking, I was wondering, *Who is this lady, and what has she done with my mother?* When I pulled up at Mother's house, I didn't see any cars. *Wow!* I thought, *Maybe she gave up the lifestyle.* I knocked on the door to the huge mansion. A lady answered the door and said, "May I help you?"

I said, "No. Where is my mother?"

"My dear, who is your mother?" the older woman asked.

"She's the owner of this house," I said as I tried to see past her.

"Sweetie, just tell me who your mother is, and then we'll go from there."

"Her name is Sandra!" I screamed, jumping up and down looking behind her.

"Oh! Miss Sandra. She's already gone for the day."

"What do you mean? Where did she go? This is her house."

"My dear, your mother works for us. This is my and my husband's home," the older woman said, as she adjusted her eyeglasses. Then, she said, "I understand now, and I see what's going on. Wait right here. Let me get my husband to help you."

She closed the door, and I walked around to the back, to the guesthouse. *This old-ass cracker must be out of her damn mind. What does she mean "my mother works for them"?* When I got to the guesthouse, I saw that the outside appeared just as I had left it. Then, I tried to open the door with my key. It didn't fit. I tried it again, but putting the key in upside down this time. *Shit! I broke one of my long nails.* I walked around to the back door, but I had no luck.

"What is going on?" I asked myself as I sat on a stone bench.

I called Mother and got no answer. I left her a voice message and headed back home doing ninety miles per hour. I had no idea what was going on. Mother wasn't answering her phone. Then, I thought, *Maybe I went to the wrong house.* But that was impossible because I lived in the guesthouse and Mother lived in the mansion. *I feel like I am losing my mind.*

When I pulled up in my neighborhood, I went straight to Cornelius's house. I walked in and didn't even knock. He was in the kitchen talking on the phone. I sat on the sofa, and I watched him as he talked on the phone. I was mesmerized by everything that he did. He hung up the phone and joined me on the sofa. Then, he kissed me and said, "I missed you last night."

I felt like I was in love with him.

"I missed you, too, but I thought that it would be best if I stayed at home. I would have hurt that damn step-daughter of yours."

"Speaking of her, she ran away last night. I was just on the phone with the police, filing a missing person's report because she's still a minor."

I stared off into space, thinking, *Good*. I hope that bitch gets hit by a Mack truck. Then, I went into character and said, "What?"

"I'm worried because it's dangerous out there."

I didn't give a fuck if she jumped off the Bay Bridge.

"I tried to plead with her and beg her to stay, but she's so feisty, and she'd already made up her mind. She told me that she never wanted to see me again in her life. And she said that she has something special to say at her mom's funeral. She said that she wants to read a poem that she's made up. But she's so angry, and now I'm starting to think that that might be a bad idea."

"I think you should bar her from the funeral."

"Are you serious? Bar her from her own mother's funeral?"

"Yes, I'm serious as a heart attack. She's only going to make a fool out of you."

"Nah, she's just taking this hard. Once this funeral is over, I think things will go back to normal. She's frustrated, and she has a lot to deal with."

"Okay. Suit yourself, and, when the time comes, I'll be sure to tell you that I told you so."

I made myself at home at his house. I had rearranged his furniture, and I helped Devin with his homework. I had slowly moved in. I had moved all his wife's pictures out of the living room, replacing them with my own. I was the head bitch in charge, and Cornelius did everything that I told him to do. I never asked him to do anything. Sinai was still gone, and I was happy.

Chapter 18:
The Funeral

It was the day of the funeral, and I was right by Cornelius's side. When we walked in the church, we were stared down by plenty of people. *Why are they looking at me and not mourning?* I looked back at them with a fake grin. I didn't care about them. I had the man of my dreams. After we viewed Cherry's body, Sinai walked up to us. She wasn't crying, and she looked like she'd been up fucking all night. Her eyeliner was running, and her hair wasn't even combed. She looked at me and said, "I'm glad you could make it." She looked at Cornelius and rolled her eyes.

"Don't worry about her," I said as we took our seats.

The preacher began his eulogy. "Cherry is gone on home to be with the Lord…"

I never understood why preachers assumed that the dead always made it to Heaven. That bitch could be in Hell frying with the devil. After he talked about Cherry's life, he changed the subject. And for some strange reason, it looked as if he was looking at me the whole time. Then, he said, "I want to talk to some of you devils in here today. And I want to focus on the young people in here today. Young folks, it's never too late to get your life in order."

He needs to be talking to Sinai, instead of talking and looking at me. I'm a grown ass woman, I thought as I looked over Cherry's obituary and read it silently. *This is a pretty picture of her.*

I was so glad when he finally shut the fuck up. I was about to lose my cool because I felt as if he was preaching to me. Then, the preacher called Sinai to the microphone. She grabbed the microphone, looked at her mother's casket, and said, "I'm doing this for you, Mama."

She looked at everyone and said, "This is a poem that I made up."

Women Are Dogs, Too

Cornelius, she's sitting right next to you.

But, boy, oh, boy, do I have a surprise for you.

I never liked you and the things you do.

Now you've moved that bitch in our home,

And we both know that she's not grown.

For crying out loud, she was a babysitter,

And now she's just plain mean and bitter.

I don't like your new friend Patience, is it?

I'm coming back home to pay you a visit

I know the real truth about my mom,

And I'm happy that y'all could come,

But I have to say this and get it off my chest.

I'll start with what's important, not mentioning the rest.

Some of you thought my mama died from cancer,

But that was a lie and the wrong answer.

She should have stayed with my daddy; they were all right,

But all they did was fuss and fight.

I hate that she had to upgrade

Because it was Cornelius who gave her AIDS.

Chapter 19:
I Don't Fight in Heels, but I Will

I could not believe my ears. Everyone in the church began to clear their throats, whisper to one another, and look around at us. When I looked at Cornelius, he was sweating bullets. I elbowed him and whispered, "What does she mean, you gave her mother AIDS?"

"She's lying. And I knew that I shouldn't have let her speak here," he said as he adjusted his necktie.

When Sinai was done making her grand speech, she dropped the microphone as if she had done something cool, but she wasn't going to walk past me after saying those things about me. As she walked by me, I stuck my leg out and tripped her up. She fell right in my lap, and her ass was mine. I grabbed her by her hair, looked her in her face, and said, "Didn't I tell you that I was the wrong one to fuck with, bitch?"

She tried swinging, but I was too quick. When I stood up, I towered over her. I was wearing the highest pair of heels that I owned. They were six inches, and I felt one of my ankles twist, but that didn't matter. I had Sinai right where I wanted her. I was on top of her, and no one could get me off. And she said, "Let me up, bitch, so I can show you what I can do."

I gave her a chance and let her stand on her two feet. And there we stood up face-to-face like two kangaroos in the wild. She started swinging wildly, and, all of a sudden, I felt the left side of my face get wet. I was bleeding. *She cut me with a razor*, I thought.

She said, "Now look who fucked with the wrong one."

I was swinging, trying to hit her, but the more I swung, the weaker I had become. Then, I felt my body collapse and hit the floor. *Why isn't anyone helping me up?* I wondered. No one tried to help get Sinai off me, not even Cornelius. She continued to slice my face with that razor.

Then, I heard a voice calling my name. "Patience! Patience! After I snap my finger three times, you'll be awake."

Snap! Snap! Snap!

I opened my eyes and saw that I was in a room, lying on a twin-sized bed. I felt my face, and there was no blood. Then, I noticed that I was handcuffed to the bed.

"Who are you? Where am I? Where is Cornelius? What is this place?"

"I'll answer all of your questions very soon," she said as she turned on the lights and closed the door. The bright lights hurt my eyes. I saw that there were several other people in the room with us, a man and a lady. I made out the lady's name tag. Her name was Ms. Kasha. She had on bright-colored scrubs, and her hair was pretty. Then, I looked at the white lady who was trying to tell me to calm down.

"Patience, I'm Dr. Hardwick, and I've had you under very deep hypnosis. It's almost like an imaginative role-enactment. And I must say, my dear, you've got quite the imagination. I'll answer all of your questions, but, before I do, I have a question for you. Are you going to be nice this time? If not, Ms. Kasha will have to inject you again?"

I looked over at Ms. Kasha, and she held up a needle.

"The last time I did this hypnosis on you, you didn't cooperate, and Ms. Kasha had to inject you. Ms. Kasha is in charge here at Georgia Regional Hospital, and she knows exactly what to do for you if you cut up. Now again, before we get started, I need to know, are you going to be nice this time?"

"Yes," I said, just so she could tell me why I was where I was.

She signaled for Ms. Kasha and the others to leave. Then, she pressed record on a tape player and said, "For the record, I will state my name. This is Dr. Debbie Hardwick with ID badge number 543-996, and I will begin my child's personality assessment on Patience Sinai Washington."

"What did you just call me? Did you call me that bitch Sinai?"

The doctor looked at me and said, "My dear, you are Sinai."

"How can that be? She just sliced my face at Cornelius's wife's funeral?"

"When I take your handcuffs off, I want you to walk over to the mirror."

She released me from the bed, and I looked in the mirror and saw that I looked just like Sinai.

"I'll give you a minute," she said as I stood there and started to cry. "It's okay, my dear."

"But what…but why? Where is Cornelius?"

"Sweetheart, there is no Cornelius. There is no Devin and Kevin, and there is no Cherry. And there is no Tiberius. They are all figments of your imagination. You are in here because you have been charged with attempted murder."

"Murder?" I said as I slouched down to the floor.

"Yes, sweetheart. Murder."

Chapter 20:
Nothing But the Truth

"Patience, do you even know why you're here?"

"No," I said as I looked at the gown that I had on. "Why am I here?"

"Why don't we do this, sweetheart? Why don't we get your mother in here?"

"My mother? But she's probably with one of her rich white clients."

She walked over to the door and in walked Mother. She didn't look like herself. She didn't have any long hair extensions in her head. And she wasn't "designered up" either. She had on a pair of white scrubs. Then, Dr. Hardwick said, "Let's note for the record that the patient's mother, Sandra Washington, is joining us." She looked at me and said, "Sweetheart, this is the part of the session where I need for you to listen only. Please don't say a word."

Mother took a seat at the brown table and looked at Dr. Hardwick and said, "How's my baby doing?"

"We have a lot more work to do. So far, I've seen many different personalities in her. And she doesn't even know the reason why she's here. So that's why I've asked you to come here. I want her to hear it coming from your mouth. I want you to take her back to that awful night when this all happened."

"Can I, at least, sit next to her?" Mother asked.

"No, that's not a good idea right now. She's still a bit confused, and she's going in and out of character."

Then, Mother looked at me with tears in her eyes. "Patience baby, first I want to let you know that I love you with all my heart. Your dad and I are praying for you. And we both love you very much. Oh, my God, I don't know where to begin. I was working for the Whiteheads, and I got the phone call that I have dreaded all my life. Your father called me. He was frantic. It all started when you were in the seventh grade. You had a great graduation, and you were on your way to middle school. Your father and I were so proud of you. And we wanted for you what any loving, caring parents would want for their daughter. We wanted you to have a great and safe summer job. I got you a babysitting job three doors down from our house. It was a good job because you could, then, afford to get your hair done every week by Vicki at OV's. Carl and Shelia Wilson were their names. They had a set of twin boys named Eric and Deric. They were three years old. You loved them boys just like you loved your Cabbage Patch kid dolls. But, for some reason, you became obsessed with Carl and jealous of Shelia. Shelia said that she'd first noticed it when she saw that someone had cut her out of their family photos. Then, she said she'd come home and find Carl's clothing packed in suitcases by the front door. She'd ask Carl if he was going on a vacation without telling her because they did everything together. She even went as far as questioning her boys. But Shelia liked you, so she kept you around. You were so good with her boys. You taught them many things. You taught them their ABCs and their colors, and you taught them how to count. And you did all of this when they were only three years old. So, anyway, one night, when Shelia came home from work, all the lights were off. She said she called your names, but she got no answer. She tried to turn on the lights, but they didn't come on. She opened up all of the windows to get some light in from the street lights. Then, she said she went to the garage to try turning them on from the breaker. Still nothing, then she said she lit some candles. She walked all over the house, looking for you and the boys. Then, she said that you attacked her with a hammer. While you were attacking her, you were saying that Carl belonged to you. You went on and on about how much you loved him. You were saying that you and Carl were moving away together.

You told her that you and Carl were going to raise their twins. You even told her that you and Carl had had sex in their bed. And Shelia said that she was begging you to put the hammer down and to tell her where the twins were. But, by that time, you'd already struck her in the arm. She was bleed profusely. 'Why are you doing this to me?' Shelia kept asking, but she said you were in rage and kept striking her with the hammer."

Chapter 21:
Where Are the Twins?

"So, when it was all over and done, your father found you in your room, in the closet, covered in blood. He was asking you what had happened, but he couldn't make out what you were saying. The only thing he said you kept repeating was that they're safe now. What does that mean, sweetheart? If the twins are safe, where are they? Did you hurt them, too, sweetheart?"

"Where is your long weave and your Fendi furs?" I asked. "And why are you dressed like a maid?"

"Patience, I am a caregiver. I work for Mr. Whitehead. I have been working for him in Duluth for the last twenty years."

Then, Dr. Hardwick interrupted and said, "Let me fill you in about that." She grabbed a notepad and began to read off of it. "Well, for starters, she thinks that she's twenty-six years old. And while under hypnosis, she seems to think that you and she are high-paid whores. She thinks that Mr.

Whitehead is a billionaire trick and that you live in a mansion while she lives in the mansion's guesthouse. She thinks that Shelia's name is Cherry. She thinks that Carl's name is Cornelius. She thinks that the twin boy's names are Kevin and Devin. She also thinks that they are nine years old. She believes that one of them is dead. She thinks that Cherry is dead, pardon me, she thinks that Shelia is dead. And she also created an alter ego for herself named Sinai. She's a seventeen-year-old troubled teen. And I find that extremely odd, considering that's her middle name, and she's seventeen as well. Usually when girls her age create an alter ego, the name doesn't stay the same. However, the attitude is always ten times worse. She has also made up an imaginary boyfriend by the name of Tiberius. Does Tiberius ring any bells? She seems to think that he's an electrician."

Mother looked at me, then glanced over at Dr. Hardwick and shook her head no.

"I am sitting right here, you know?" I said as I stared at Mother's clothing.

Dr. Hardwick said, "My dear, we know you are, and it's important that you hear all of this. Do you understand what your mother just said? Do you understand what I just said?"

"I don't understand any of this. I want to go back home to Cornelius."

"Sweetheart, there is no Cornelius," Dr. Hardwick said. "I'm trying to figure out your real personality. I need to know where the twin boys are. Shelia and Carl didn't press any charges. But, honey, the state picked up the case, and you are being charged with attempted murder. Shelia lost one of her arms, but she forgives you. We need to know what you did with the twins. So, under this next hypnosis, instead of you telling me your story, I'll do it differently this time. I'll ask you the same question over and over in different ways. Can you handle that, Patience?"

I looked over at Mother, and she had her hand over her mouth. Then, she said, "We need you to speak up. We need to hear your side of the story. It's been two days, and I'm doing everything I can to keep you from going to jail. Your father and I miss you so much, and we want to put this behind us and bring you home. You have family and friends that love and miss you, as well. Your best friend Sunflower has been worried sick about you. We were a happy family once upon a time. Don't you remember? Here look at these photos; Mr. Whitehead was kind enough to have you a Little Mermaid-themed birthday party for your sixth birthday. You were so happy, and this was the best day of your life. Here's a picture of your dad holding you."

I looked at the pictures and saw that my face was painted. And I was dressed as the Little Mermaid. *That was my favorite cartoon growing up*, I thought.

"Here's another one," she said. "You and I were skating at Golden Glide skating rink. We went there every weekend, and that was our mother-daughter quality time together. Do you remember this, Patience? You were nine years old right here. Do you remember those Little Mermaid skates? You were crazy about Little Mermaid. Oh, sweetheart, say something. You don't remember any of this? Here. Why don't you take them all?" Mother said as she handed me more pictures. "Maybe they'll trigger something in your memory. It's killing me to see you like this," Mother said as she walked away in tears.

Then, I spoke slowly and said, "I remember that night, and it wasn't how Mother explained it at all, and I have proof."

Chapter 22:
Patience Speaks

I knew that I needed to speak up and tell the truth. But what I couldn't figure out was why I had to be under so much medicine. Dr. Hardwick had said that Ms. Kasha had given me several shots. I didn't need those shots. I was being very cooperative. It was all coming back to me now. I remembered that, right before the shot was given, Ms. Kasha was accompanied by a man. And that man was Carl.

I cleared my throat and said, "I remember that night like it was yesterday. But, first, let me say this. I didn't need those damn shots. And I don't need any more hypnosis. I am very clear, and I know what happened. I may have a slight problem. But hell who doesn't? And I'm almost sure that Carl is trying to set me up. You don't understand now, but you will once you hear my side.

"On the night in questioned, I had just put the twins to bed. I had first noticed something different in the twins a few weeks prior. Whenever Carl, their dad, came around they were very distant, and they were under me all the time. And since Shelia worked damn near from sun up to sun down, they only had me to care for them. So my job was to watch the twins while Carl started his so-called work from home business. They never wanted me to leave them. So I decided to watch the security camera that I had installed in their house."

"Security camera?" Dr. Hardwick said.

"Yes, security camera. Now, will you just listen only please?"

"Sure. Go right ahead, but we need to confiscate that video," Dr. Hardwick said.

"The video and the twins are in a safe place. Now again, I only need your ears. I'm starting to think that you're on their side."

"Whose side?" Mother said.

"It doesn't matter. You just make sure they don't inject me with any more of those shots. So anyway I looked at the video camera, and, as sure as the sky is blue, Carl was masturbating in front of the boys. And he even had the nerve to pull on their private parts, too. It was very disturbing. And he didn't seem to care that his boys were upset and crying. And I had it in my heart to kill him that night. It seems like white folks are always doing some ill shit like that to their own kids. I wanted to do something to him right then and there. But I knew that I had to get the twins out of the house. They were too young to speak or even know that what was happening to them was wrong, for that matter. I cried and my heart went out to the twins. I loved them like they were my little brothers. I finally stopped crying and got myself together. So before I confronted him, I called Sunflower and her mom to come and get the twins and the videotape. Carl was in his office doing only God knows what. I turned the alarm off and got the twins dressed. When Sunflower and her mom came to the door, I gave them the twins and the videotape. I told Sunflower's mom not to do anything until she heard from me again. After I closed the door and saw them off, I noticed that all of the lights were off, so I opened all the blinds so that the street lights could shine in. As I walked to the living room, Carl was sitting in the recliner. Then, I said, 'I know what you've been doing to the twins, and you won't get away with it.' Then, out of nowhere, he charged at me with a hammer, but I was too quick for him.

"He said, 'You should mind your own business, you little black bitch. What I do in my household is my business.' Now, keep in mind, he's chasing me all over their house like a maniac. I was taking cover behind furniture. Then, he said, 'The pictures weren't enough. I thought for sure that Shelia would have fired your black ass by now.' 'Why would I cut

Shelia out of her own family photos? You are one sick motherfucker, and, if I get my hands on that hammer, you're dead. And furthermore why would I have an obsession for you?' I said as I dodged a swing. 'You're an unattractive-ass white man, and I like boys my age. You're no David Bechkam. Hell! You're not even Eminem.' Then, we heard Shelia come in, and I quickly said, 'Help! I'm in the living room with your crazy ass husband.' She didn't hear what I'd said because I heard her say, 'What's going on with the lights?' So apparently she went to turn them on from the breaker in the garage. Then, the lights came on, and she walked in. I was behind the sofa, and Carl had disappeared. 'We got to get out of here,' I said. 'Carl has been doing some very bad things to the twins. I have it all on videotape. And he just tried to attack me with a hammer!' 'Hold up, sweetheart! What do you mean?' she asked as she hung up her coat. 'I mean, he has been molesting them.' I looked at her, and she didn't seem upset. So I knew that I had to get my black ass out of that house. She knew what was going on. She said, 'First, tell me where the videotape is, and it'll all be over.' But I knew I couldn't trust her either.

"'Look, lady. I just told you that your husband has been molesting your twin boys.' 'I heard you loud and clear,' she said as she ran after me. 'You should mind your own business; those are just fun home videos for us to watch when we get bored.' I've continued to let you work for us, so you wouldn't become another pregnant teen. Your mom told me all about your promiscuity. So I felt sorry for your little black ass. Now, I wish that I'd let you become another statistic.' 'So what? My mom told you about me being promiscuous. That's any typical teenager.' I tried to run past her, but Carl met me at the door.

Chapter 23:
My Prognosis

"Carl grabbed me, and then he shoved me over to Shelia. He said, 'Hold her very still. We're going to get rid of her. You don't want to give up the videotape? We'll just make this look like you tried to kill my wife.' 'But what about your twins?' I said. 'I'm the only one who knows where they are.' He said, 'I know that they're with Sunflower. I overheard your whole conversation, and I will get them back.' I started moving around, trying to get out of Shelia's hold. She held me tight as he swung the hammer at me. I wiggled like a worm, and that was when I heard Shelia gasp. He'd hit her instead of me. I ran out of the house, and that was why I was covered with her blood, so you see, I'm not the one who had the hammer. And that's how she got struck with the hammer. And it's all on video. There's a small camera on their curtain rod in the living room. All of this is captured, and you'll see that I'm innocent."

"That's great, sweetheart," Mother said, relieved from stress.

Dr. Hardwick, then, went to the telephone to put an APB out on Carl. As Mother came over to hug me, she said, "I knew that you'd tell the truth. And I'm sorry I ever doubted you. You're so smart and strong. Your father and I only wanted what we thought was best for you."

Then, all of a sudden, alarms and sirens started going off. We all looked at each other. Mother grabbed me and pulled me close to her, and Dr. Hardwick locked the door. No one knew what was going on. Then, an officer came to the door and said that he and his colleagues had caught Mr. Wilson. He'd been dressed as a doctor and had been trying to make his way to us. We all were relieved that he was caught. They brought charges on them both, him and Sheila.

"So now what?" I asked as I looked at Dr. Hardwick and Mother. "Well, it looks as if all charges will be dropped against you."

She handed me a bag of clothes. "Get dressed, and I'll tell you my prognosis. However, young lady, you do have some things that are not quite right with you."

"Oh, you mean because I'm a Gemini, and I have quite the imagination, right? I have to admit. Sometimes, my mind can get a little twisted."

She said, "Well, it's all a figment of your imagination, and, sweetheart, this has nothing to do with zodiac signs." Then, she looked at Mother and said, "I highly recommend that she seek counseling and be put on medication. I am giving you my professional opinion and some motherly advice. I'll continue seeing you for treatment, which will include putting you under hypnosis. You have a condition called DID, which is also known as dissociative personality disorder. It's common in people who have had a history of trauma. And I know that there is some trauma in your past. Psychotherapy is generally considered to be the main component of treatment for DID. I'll write you a prescription for anxiety as well. It's very clear to me that when you were under hypnosis you create several different people in your head. And there's nothing wrong with that because you have suffered some trauma. Now, would you like to tell me what that was?"

I looked at her with tears in my eyes and told her that I had witnessed my boyfriend Courtney's murder.

"What?" Mother blurted out.

Dr. Hardwick put up her hand to silence Mother and said, "No, this is good. Let her finish."

"Mother, I never told you this, but, about two years ago, I did have a boyfriend, and we were very much in love. His name was Courtney, and he was twenty-one years old.

He was from New Orleans. He had moved here with his cousin. So let's just say that his past haunted him. He had told me that he had been involved in some gang activity. He also told me that he'd done some bad things, such as rob and shoot people. You know things of that nature. He was in a gang, and it showed, too. He had tattoos everywhere, including his face. But I didn't care about none of that. All I wanted was him. He was dark brown with a curly afro. I loved running my fingers through his hair. So, one day, when we were leaving the mall, I noticed that he seemed different. He was very observant. It seemed like we were riding for hours, and he finally pulled over on a dead end street and said, 'This car has been following us since we left the mall.' He told me not to look back. Then, he grabbed my face and kissed me. He said that he loved me and that he'd be right back. But before he could even get out of the car, guns were drawn on both sides. As he tried to reach for his gun under the seat, it was too late. The guy on his side had pulled the trigger and blown his brains out, killing him instantly. Then, the guy said to him, 'That's for killing my brother.' Then, the guy on my side said, 'This has nothing to do with you. That motherfucker killed our older brother, and we've been praying for this day to come.' I grabbed him and rocked back and forth, telling him that I loved him. There was blood all over the windshield. I called 911, but I couldn't give a description of the killers. It had all happened so fast, but it seemed like it took forever for the police to get there. I had to sit there in the car with Courtney's dead body. I was traumatized, and, while sitting there, I saw his pink brains sliding down the windshield. I wanted to get out and run, but I didn't know where the killers were. The policeman finally came and notified his next of kin, and that was the last time I ever saw Courtney."

"Awww...sweetheart. I'm sorry that you had to witness such a horrific crime," Mother said.

Then, as she wrote on a piece of paper, Dr. Hardwick said, "Well, that explains who Cornelius is. It's normal for people with DID, who have experienced that type of trauma. You've created this happy life with Cornelius to block out the actual murder that you witnessed of Courtney. But, sweetheart, it's perfectly understandable, and you'll be just fine." She tore a prescription from her pad. She handed it to me and said that she wanted to see me every two weeks. I was relieved that I had gotten it all out. I didn't want to relive my past, but I was glad that Dr. Hardwick had dug deep into my mind. I called Sunflower, and her mom brought the twins to the nearest police precinct. The twins were released to Shelia's sister. She said that she had never trusted Carl and that she believed that Shelia had been coerced into doing those awful things to the twins. She said that the Shelia she knew would have never done such a thing. Mother thanked Dr. Hardwick for all that she had done for me. Then, Mother said, "Come on, sweetheart. Let's go home…where you belong."

About The Author

    Antoinette Tunique Smith was born in San Francisco, California and raised in ATL, where she still resides. She is blessed with five children who are known as the five lights of her life: Pinky, Driah, Clyde, Chicken and Fat Boy.

    She would like people to know that it doesn't matter where you come from, you can be whatever you wanna be. Just believe in God. There is a God!

Thanks & Much
respect,
Antoinette Smith

AND PLEASE CHECK OUT ANTOINETTE'S
PREVIOUSLY RELEASED BOOKS:

*DADDY'S FAVORITE POP
*MARRIED: SNEAKY BLACK WOMAN
*WHITE COP, LIL' BLACK GURL
*I'M A DRAG, NOT A FAG
"BLACKOUT ON BANKHEAD"

AND PLEASE STAY TUNED FOR ANTOINETTE'S UPCOMING
BOOKS:

I'M BI WHY LIE?
TREY AND HIS DNA (SEQUEL TO I'M A DRAG, NOT A FAG)
I WISH I WAS RAISED (MY LIFE'S STORY)
MY FATHER'S SEED (SEQUEL TO DADDY'S FAVORITE POP)
MARRIED, SNEAKY BLACK MAN (SEQUEL TO MARRIED, SNEAKY
BLACK WOMAN)

I really hope you guys enjoy my Straight to the Point Books!!

Reader Comments

From
straighttothepointbooks.com:

Stacey Mobley-Cook – Tampa, Fl. - 3/19/13
I had the pleasure of reading Im a Drag Not A Fag and White Cop Little Black Girl. I truly enjoyed both books.They are well written, grabs your attention from begining to end. I just purchased Married Sneaky Black Woman and Daddy's Favorite Pop I'm sure that I will enjoy them both Keep up the good work

Natasha Parker – United States. - 3/13/13
Please Check this author out..any of Antoinette Smith Books will blow ya mind..It's hard to put the book down becus the stories gets straight to the point!!

Lashonda Jeffries – Atlanta, Ga. - 3/11/13
I love all your books friend. In married sneaky black women i called u a million times wondering how you come up with this stuff. You motive me to the fullest . Love you keep it going

Shacoria Tukes – College Park, GA. - 3/10/13
I must say I didn't like reading at first. My mom told me to read the 1st page of DADDY'S FAVORITE POP...OMG I couldn't put it down! OUTSTANDING, I take my hat off to you. I have read all four of your books. Now I'm waiting on BLACK OUT ON BANKHEAD!

Angela Tukes – Georgia. - 3/10/13
I am a true reader, and must say that you did that, AWESOME! Every book from the 1st to your latest. Keep them coming MAMI. You are a beautiful talented BLACK WOMAN! I know I'm not the only one waiting on a movie...TYLER PERRY WHERE YOU AT!!

Melinda 'Pooh' Pressley – Riverdale, Ga. - 3/07/13

I had the pleasure of meeting Antoinette years before she wrote these books and she told myself and my family her story. And her story inspired her to write 'Daddy's Favorite Pop'. When I read that book I could not put that book down. I rode to Alabama one day and read the entire book and called her with question and asked when the next book comes out. Then here comes 'Married Sneaky Black Woman' it was like a mystery I couldn't go to sleep until I finished reading the damn book. I called her and said "damn u clever as hell" when the next book come out! Then she put out ' White Cop, Lil Black Gurl' man on man.... That was good... I called her up and said next. She put out I'm a Drag not a Fag' this book was so unique. People I am Antoinette Smith #1 fan with the hood books. If she don't hurry up with Black-Out on Bankhead Imma screammmmm!!! Antoinette I love you and keep up the good work. I will see you in the big legend soon!

(DIVA) Michelle Powell – Stone Mountain, Ga. - 2/26/13

I have read Daddy's Favorite Pop.. That was my Favorite that book made me want to read more..Then I read Married Sneaky Black Woman..That book was very Interesting I cant wait to read Pt. 2.. I also read White Cop Little Black Girl.. I don't thin I could have done time I liked that one too. I've read I'm a DRAG Not A Fag..OMG Now that book there I couldn't put It down I went on a Weekend vacation and I read this book two days.. I'm waiting on pt. 2 of Daddy's Favorite Pop.. Just to let you know Antoinette I (DIVA) Am your # 1 Fan I Intend to purchase all of your books as they come out I want the whole Collection. Your are the best writer in my book..Keep them coming PEACE AND LOVE DIVA

TaShanna Word – Journey - 10/23/12

Amazing......You are truly gifted and blessed. I did not put your book down Daddy's Favorite Pop. Can't wait to read the others. I've worked *in the social service field for over 15 yrs. I have heard and seen some of the worst cases in my career. Ms. Smith, I would love to have lunch and see if you are able to speak with the teens that are on my case load. Survivor you are and your Future get ready for it ....*

Ed Weathers – College Park, Ga. - 8/27/12

I love your books because they talk about real every day people, people you may see on the train or the street and also you help people get there voice out there no matter what.

Sharon LadeeStorem Acres – Atlanta, Ga. - 8/04/12

My name is Sharon {Ladee Storem} Acres and I met you at Big Daddy's soul food place off of Riverdale a few years back and you gave me your card. I have a Radio Show call Claim Your Fame Radio Show on WAEC Love 860 AM in Atlanta Ga and we reach 5 to 6 million listeners, I would love for you to be on the show. My website is www.storemandsun.com or call Storem and Sun Ent. at 678-268-7859

Kaliliah– Atlanta, Ga. - 6/26/12

OMG...This author never cease to amaze me! Excellent writer with amazing story lines! "I'm a drag not a fag" is most definitely a must read. I couldn't stop...I had to get to the end! Keep up the good work Antoinette!! You will always have my support!!

Rosey – United States - 4/27/12

KUDOS to you and your hard work and tremendous success! Keep on going girlfriend... you inspire me ;) All the Best ~Rosey

Tarsha Latrice – College Park, Ga. - 4/04/12

I read your first book and loved it!! Just got my copy of the second book and will start reading tonight!! keep doing your thang....I love your hustle!!!

www.straighttothepointbooks.com
acansing2000@yahoo.com